GW01417968

The Meeting House

A short story collection

OAKMAGIC PUBLICATIONS

First published in 2008 by
OAKMAGIC PUBLICATIONS
1 Sir Williams Lane
Aylsham
Norwich NR11 6AW

i

THE MEETING HOUSE

Grateful acknowledgement is made to Anglian Maintenance Ltd (Contracting & General Building Work) for their financial support.

ISBN: 978-190433-069-1

Printed in England on FSC-approved paper by www.printondemand-worldwide.com

The Meeting House
Contents

Foreword

I deally, a writer should be haunted. Haunted by ideas, characters and especially settings.

As a crime and fantasy writer, I have come to believe that. And I also believe that the best writing of all is a kind of haunting. The stories we remember best are those which linger in our imaginations like old ghosts, refuse to leave our waking thoughts, embed themselves in our subconscious, burst forth from our memories years later. So that on occasions we may even dream of them.

The stories in this anthology each have something of that quality about them. They are the work of a small group of people who have met each week for a period of some two years in the small town of Aylsham. Each has taken a substantial risk: to plunge into his or her subconscious, to dredge up an idea, then fashion and mould it into a recognisable shape, breathe life into it. To do that is no easy task. To be an effective writer takes great and constant practice. Writing does not fit well with the age of celebrity status, endless distraction and instant gratification. It is an activity always challenging, sometimes frustrating and frequently disappointing. And it is best practised for the right reasons: not for an ambition to achieve instant fame and popularity but to shape a story into life for its own sake; to beat and bend it into a living entity. Writing is therefore a deeply unfashionable activity for the twenty first century.

The writers represented here are aware of that fact. They are unknown to the reading public, yet I believe their work deserves an audience. They have certain qualities in common. They all live within a short radius of Norwich; they all share an enthusiasm for and love of words; they are committed to their craft.

Their stories – and some of them have written few or no stories before – range widely in subject matter and content and there is no common theme. In this volume there are tales of human tragedy and perversity; murder, love and the supernatural; of time past, present and future.

Above all, they show an emphasis on characterisation and the foibles of human nature. They demonstrate to us that life can often be puzzling, unpredictable, amusing or downright disastrous.

As their tutor, it has been my privilege to help tend their gardens, to watch as the dreams have taken shape from beyond the veil of the conscious mind, to assist from the sidelines as the project has slowly gathered momentum and shape. The greatest obstacle for those wishing to write is always the suspension of disbelief; principally of disbelief in oneself. But once the journey has begun and the scornful self - critic relegated to the doorstep, it is often surprising what emerges from that deep well of the unconscious mind.

As these writers have discovered, writing is a journey. And it is also a kind of dreaming aloud. These stories demonstrate how the dream can function on many levels and haunt us to distraction.

So, dear reader, time to suspend your disbelief and dive into the pool. Turn off the TV, disconnect the phone, and begin.

Kelvin I. Jones

Jack Andrews

Jack Andrews, retired photo-journalist and son of a
professional footballer, has lived in Drayton for many years
with his wife Anne and Leo, a near psychotic Siamese cat.
On newspaper assignments he covered national stories and
events including the Hindley/Brady moors murders, the
Belfast troubles and many Royal occasions.
Other interests include all sports, DIY and aspirations to
write a short film script.

Jack Andrews

Reminiscent of story from one of the Boys 1950s/60s Annuals eg. Rover, Wizzard etc.

A shrill blast of the referee's whistle signalled half-time and the stocky figure of Steve Bayliss strode quickly from the dusty cinder pitch, leaving his Hardy Street team-mates in his wake. He was angry at the mediocre performance his team had displayed so far, but mostly at himself. He had missed a golden chance to put his side ahead in the final minutes of the half.

It was semi-finals night of the annual seven-a-side football competition, sponsored by the local evening newspaper. For all the young players taking part, none of them a day over fourteen, this was the pinnacle of their season, their chance to carry the banner for dads, older brothers or uncles who had seen their own dreams of turning out for Liverpool or Everton disappear with their youth. Nothing in the city's sporting calendar generated so much fierce pride as the respective street teams battled for the much coveted trophy.

The competition had commenced in the early 1950's, the brainchild of the newspaper's Sports Editor, and was centred on the Anfield and Kirkdale districts of Liverpool . Competing teams were all drawn from the densely packed streets that crisscrossed these well - populated areas. The make-shift pitches were flattened cinder covered rectangles set amid the endless rows of red brick terraced houses, each with its well scrubbed front doorstep and pristine white curtains. Here and there were large gaps between the dwellings like missing teeth. Each gap, like the pitch, was a legacy of the vicious wartime bombing raids on the city.

During the interval the players, enjoying segments of thirst quenching oranges, found their blue and white sweat-soaked shirts beginning to cool in the chilly evening air, making several shiver. Each of them was quietly locked into his own private thoughts, oblivious to snippets of advice being tendered by well-meaning neighbours and supporters. There had been no score in the first half and they were all disappointed with their showing. They had been knocked out in the semi-finals the previous season and every player desperately wanted to go one stage further this year. But first they had to get past tonight's opponents, Fernie Grove, a tough side to beat.

Gathering his team around him, Steve told them in no uncertain terms what was expected of them. They all knew it would require a big improvement during the remaining thirty minutes of the game if they wanted to progress to the final.

As the sky darkened and rain began to drizzle the referee walked to the centre of the pitch. The rain did not affect the spectators too much, then their chattering took on a sharper edge of expectation before exploding into wild cheering and clapping as the teams trotted back. A determined Steve Bayliss, clapping his hands loudly, shouted to his team.

'Come on lads, get stuck in, let's play' em off the park.' Chants of Hard-y Street , Hard-y Street were matched by shouts of encouragement from the Fernie Grove followers. The loud vocal support, accompanied by an ear splitting noise of wooden rattles echoed from the surrounding dwellings.

Within two minutes of the restart there was near disaster for Steve's team as Fernie Grove came very close to taking the lead. In a fluent movement, one of the Grove forwards gathered the ball, turned and crashed his shot against the post with the keeper well beaten, the rebound being hurriedly booted out of play.

'Get a grip,' screamed Steve as the ball curled into the goal mouth from the resultant corner kick. Keeper Jack Wilkes leapt high to catch the swirling ball despite a strong challenge from two of the opposition. He hung on grittily, giving his colleagues vital seconds to recover.

After that narrow escape the Hardy Street boys settled down a little, but their opponents, when pressed, were tackling recklessly and gave away several fouls. From one such infringement the best chance of the game arose - and it fell to Steve. The free kick was pushed ten yards in front of him, leaving a clear run at the Grove goal, but as he sprinted forward, Billy Glen, the Fernie Grove captain, was also quickly off the mark. Billy was a big lad for his age, but extremely fast, and he soon caught up. Steve, who could now hear his opponents' feet pounding alongside of him, hesitated briefly. At the same moment as he attempted to shoot for goal Billy tackled him hard and the pair crashed down in a cloud of choking dust, each gasping with pain as the rough cinders bit into their knees and elbows. Steve got to his feet slowly and the bitter realization of what had happened in those few moments struck him. In the last few strides before the tackle he had slackened his pace as the fear of pain or injury overcame his will to win the ball - in short, he had `chickened out'.

This brief self-analysis was instantly blotted out as a vociferous roar from the crowd almost drowned out the sound of the referee's whistle, but he was clearly pointing to the spot, awarding Hardy Street a penalty. Jimmy Sellars, the youngest and smallest player in the side, had been tripped as he dribbled the ball toward their opponent's goal. He took the spot kick himself, firmly planting the ball in the back of the Grove net to the delight of his team-mates and their ecstatic supporters. The few remaining minutes of the match felt like a lifetime, the final whistle greeted by each of the Hardy Street team with a mixture of sheer joy - and some relief.

As players and spectators left the arena, emotions contrasted markedly. At one end, excited Hardy Street followers noisily voiced their delight, while their counterparts, trying to hide their disappointment, quietly moved away from the other. Surrounded by a large group of supporters, Steve, Jimmy Sellars and Jack Wilkes, were slowly edging away from the pitch when Steve spotted his dad on the fringe of the crowd. He grinned broadly, gave the thumbs up sign and joined him. Mr Bayliss playfully ruffled his lad's hair.

'Well done son, your team did us all proud out there tonight, but you didn't half leave it late getting the winner.' Slipping his arm around the boy's shoulder they continued to talk about the match as they headed home. Shouts of Champions and We're going to win the cup could still be heard echoing around the streets as darkness fell and the street gas lamps flickered on, casting their yellow light across the now empty arena. Turning the corner into Hardy Street , they noticed a light flutter on in an upstairs window above Tom Barber's shoe repair shop.

'He was at the match tonight you know Steve,' said Mr Bayliss, nodding in the direction of the shop.

'I was talking with him during the second half and did he get excited when the goal went in. He's a really nice bloke and he certainly knows his football,' Steve quietly commented.

'I can't understand why some of the local lads make fun of him and call him horrible names just because he has a gammy leg.' They had reached their front door and Mr Bayliss replied over his shoulder:

'That's typical of some youngsters today, lad, but I don't think it really bothers Tom too much anyway.'

Alone in his bedroom the following morning, Steve halfheartedly tried to catch up with some homework, but couldn't concentrate. Any thoughts of schoolwork were interrupted when his mother asked him to collect her shoes from Tom's shop. Hurriedly pushing aside his books, Steve bounded down the stairs and within minutes was opening the door of the cobbler's workshop. A large bell attached to an antiquated brass spring, fixed to the door, jangled noisily. Tom Barber, almost hidden behind a strong leather apron that reached from just below his chin to the tops of his boots, was hunched over a rackety belt driven machine which he switched off on hearing the bell. Looking up from his task, his tanned, deeply lined face immediately creased into a warm smile as he greeted the boy.

'Good morning, young Steve. I suppose you've come for your mam's shoes?' Steve nodded a yes and Tom started rummaging under the counter, re-emerging after a few moments with the shoes which he wrapped in brown paper, then handed them over the dusty counter.

'What did you think of the match last night, Mr Barber?' Steve said. Pausing momentarily, his gnarled hands still on the parcel, the cobbler replied:

'It was good - very good in parts, but you should have had the game won long before you did. I'm talking in particular about the easy chance that fell to you in the second half.' The old man's bluntness wasn't expected, and it hurt and embarrassed Steve. His face reddened noticeably.

'I suppose I should have scored shouldn't I? It was...' Tom cut short the boy's reply.

'Look son, in my younger days I knew a player who did exactly what you did out there last night. He tried to avoid a tackle instead of going flat out for the ball and he ended up with his leg being broken so badly that it put him out of the game for good - and he was a professional, that was his living. When it's a fifty-fifty ball, just you and the other fella, the one who 'chickens out' will nearly always get the worst of it, believe me. Many people only meet a moment of truth once or twice in a lifetime, but like all sportsmen, a footballer must be prepared to meet these situations in every match he plays.' The old man carried on:

'You have to show courage and the will to win every time. You'll get plenty of knocks and bruises, but the one who has the guts to see the moment through will always be a winner. It's all in the game lad; it's all part of the game.' Steve hadn't moved from the dust-laden counter while Tom had been speaking. He just stood there avoiding the old man's gaze, silently staring down at the floor. He felt guilty and a little ashamed, knowing that Tom knew the real reason for him missing last night's scoring chance.

Several seconds elapsed in complete silence before he raised his head to look directly into the old man's eyes.

'Thanks Mr Barber, you can be certain of one thing though, I won't let it happen again.' Paying for the shoes, he turned to open the shop door and as the bell jangled again he just managed to hear Tom call out:

'Good luck in the final, son.' Without turning, the boy raised his hand in acknowledgement before walking across to his home.

The days leading up to the match dragged by slowly, but it gave Steve a lot of time to reflect on what Tom Barber had said to him. His schoolwork suffered because he couldn't focus on such mundane matters as Maths and English; there were too many thoughts about Friday's final bouncing around in his head. The game, against the favourites for the competition, Gunton Close, would be the most important match the Hardy Street team had played in so far, but one thought was common to all that were to take part. This was `The' match, the `Big one', and they were going to give their all in skill and effort.

Wednesday arrived accompanied by more rain. His nose pressed against the bedroom window, Steve watched the tiny globules strike the glass and slowly lengthen before joining with other rivulets speeding down to the bottom of the wooden frame. The pavements, stone sets and roof slates were glistening wet from the constant drizzle, making the surroundings grey and miserable. However, the youngster's mind dwelt on other things - in particular his conversation with the old cobbler. Nothing was going to dampen his enthusiasm, not even the weather.

Leaving the house he spotted Jimmy Sellars and another team member, Ian MacDonald, and joined them on their way to school. They chattered constantly about the match.

They were experiencing similar feelings; a confused mixture of excitement at the possibility of winning the cup, while trying to blot out any thought of defeat. Their chirpy surface expressions only thinly disguised the jumble of nerves that each of them was encountering. The day moved along boringly and it was a relief to escape through the school gates at the end of the afternoon.

The topic of conversation on the homeward trek was Chris Reilly, the Gunton Close centre-forward. Steve and Jimmy were well aware of Chris. They all played in the same school team, and knew that he had recently been selected for the Liverpool Schoolboys squad, he was that good.

Reaching the corner of Hardy Street their discussion was halted as the bell in the cobbler's shop clanged. Tom Barber called to Steve from the doorway.

'Can you spare a moment Steve?' The youngster walked across and entered the shop, wondering why he had been called. Tom waited until the echo of the belt had faded away before asking Steve to sit down on the stool behind the counter.

'I watched this Gunton Close team in the semi-final before yours last week and although they won well in the end, during the first ten minutes they were very jittery indeed. If you can go at them hard right from the kick-off you might nick an early goal, and in a final that's worth two at any other time.' Steve listened intently to every word as the old man went on.

'Now their centre-half is a fine hefty lad and he'll gobble up any ball you put in the air near his goal, but his weakness is in his footwork, especially on the left side. He tackles like a tiger when anyone tries to pass him down his right, but on the other side he flounders a bit.' The youngster began to realize that the old man obviously knew a great deal more about football than many would have given him credit for. Absolutely spellbound he continued to listen.

'Their centre-forward is more than useful as well. If he had been given better service he would have had a bagful of goals instead of just the two he did score.' Steve knew he was referring to Chris Reilly and told him they knew about his talent and the danger he posed. The brief chat was brought to a close as Tom extended his hand, and they clasped firmly.

'Don't forget what I told you a few days ago. That's even more important. Now go out there on Friday and bring the cup back for the street.' This time there were no guilty feelings or embarrassment.

'I'll remember Tom, and we'll do our very best I promise you.' Crossing the street, Steve realised he had used Tom's first name for the first time and it seemed to emphasize the bond that had grown between them in only a few days.

Throughout teatime Steve had been unusually quiet and thoughtful, a fact his father commented on after the table had been cleared. His son then told him of his chats with Tom Barber and the advice he had been given. His dad smiled knowingly.

'There is no better person in the district qualified to give you that sort of advice son.' The boy looked puzzled.

'Why, dad?' Mr Bayliss began to explain.

'At the bus depot the other day we were talking about football in general when somewhere in the conversation Tom's name cropped up. One of the older inspectors knew of him when he played for Newcastle United in the early

1920's. His nickname then was 'Sandy' Barber because of his shock of red hair.' Steve listened spellbound.

'At that time Sandy was reckoned to be one of the best centre-forwards in the game. During the F.A.Cup semi-final against Notts County he had already scored twice when tragedy struck as he attempted to get his hat trick. Racing for the ball with an opposing defender, he went down under a heavy tackle and was stretchered off with a badly broken leg. His team went on to win the cup at Wembley, but Sandy never played again. In those days if you didn't play in the final you didn't receive a cup winner's medal and it must have devastated poor old Tom at the time.' Steve, who had been listening in complete silence until then, suddenly jumped up.

'Of course, everything fits into place. I should have guessed he'd had something important to do with the game, he knows so much about it.' His father nodded in agreement.

'If you tell some of your mates the reason Tom limps so badly, perhaps they will stop taking the mickey and begin showing him some respect.' Steve promised he would tell his pals everything before the match.

It was mid-morning when Mr Bayliss, in the middle of attempting to repair his bicycle, remembered he had promised to take a book to Jim Wilson, a driver colleague at the depot. Bolts, nuts, spanners and washers were strewn over several sheets of newspaper on the floor of the front parlour, and he didn't particularly want to abandon the job. As his school was being used as a local election polling booth that day and he was free, Steve volunteered to do the errand. Accepting the offer, his dad warned him to be careful as it had only just stopped raining and the roads would still be a bit slippery.

Ten minutes later, on the return journey, the accident happened. Trying to avoid a toddler who ran into the road, the front wheel of Steve's bike slid into one of the old tramlines. The cycle wobbled precariously and with its momentum instantly halted, it threw him over the handlebars, landing with a sickening thud on his knee and shoulder before sliding into the gutter on the wet greasy road. Several passers-by rushed over as he lay dazed and winded by the kerb. Recovering slowly, Steve thanked his helpers, at the same time surveying the buckled front wheel and twisted handlebars of his bicycle. As he made a closer inspection of the damage he began to feel the pain and increasing stiffness in his knee and shoulder. He then noticed a great tear in his trousers and he knew his mother wouldn't be best pleased when she saw it.

Nearly an hour had passed before he pushed the damaged bike through the back door, where he was greeted by his mother.

'What in heaven's name has happened to you? Are you alright? Look at the state of your trousers.' Mr Bayliss joined them in the kitchen as they waited for their son to explain.

'I just had a tumble off the bike, it was those `blinkin' old tramlines in Kirkdale Road. I wish they'd get rid of them.'

'Have you hurt yourself?' said his father.

'My knee feels a bit sore, that's all.' There was no way he was about to tell his dad that he'd hurt his shoulder as well.

Back in his room, Steve stripped off the torn trousers and was shocked to see the extent of the swelling around his knee. Apart from being badly grazed and cut, the colour was rapidly changing from red to an angry purple, and his shoulder was creating even more discomfort. However, the greatest fear uppermost in his mind was whether he would be able to play the following evening. He began to panic a little, and then recalled his mother wrapping his ankle in a series of cold water compresses when he had fallen in the street some years before. Limping to the bathroom, he locked himself in. He carefully sponged the swollen knee over and over again and it began to ease the pain and reduce the swelling. He continued this process for a further ten minutes, until his mother shouted from the bottom of the stairs for his torn trousers.

'I'll be down in a minute mam,' he called, rummaging in the first-aid box for a bandage. Returning to his room he changed into a tracksuit, gathered up the ripped trousers, and gingerly made his way downstairs. His dad had finished repairing his bike and was about to go out to test it.

'I suppose you'll want me to have a look at your wreck of a bike now?' Steve nodded a yes. Handing the trousers to his mother he quickly made for the front door saying that he wanted to speak to some of the team. In truth he had somewhere else to go first.

He headed straight for Tom's shop and caught him as he was about to lock up for the day. Tom was surprised to see the boy there, but at Steve's bidding he slid back the door bolts and let him in, reaching up to stifle the bell.

'What's the matter? What's wrong lad?' Steve started to explain as he revealed the damage to his leg. Tom's eyebrows knitted together in a deep frown on seeing the swollen joint.

'You've given it a very nasty bang, that's for sure, but you did the right thing with the cold water.'

'What can I do Tom? I don't want to miss the match.' The old man stood silent for a moment then sprang into action.

'Wait here.' Tom walked through the workshop and upstairs to his living quarters. Steve could hear him moving about between the rooms above him before reappearing with a hand towel over his shoulder, a wide bandage and an old ribbed glass bottle containing a brownish liquid. Before the boy could ask what was in the bottle, Tom said: 'I'm going to rub this stuff on your knee and when it gets into the cuts it will hurt like hell and sting for a long time, but I promise you it will help.' Steve didn't look too keen but was prepared to accept anything if it would give him the chance of playing. He sat on the counter and Tom began to massage his knee and leg. The sharp stinging pain took his breath away making him wince, but the old man continued without appearing to notice the agonized expression on the boy's face. A strong smell of liniment filled the air in the shop. Steve's eyes began to water and he asked what the brown stuff was.

'It's a mixture of horse liniment and olive oil son, an old fashioned method of relieving stiff limbs; don't ask me what makes it work, but it does. As a matter of fact I still use it often, it eases the pain in my legs.' He wiped his hands on the towel and applied the wide bandage around the boy's knee.

'This is a crepe bandage which will stay tight and should see you through tomorrow's game, but the important thing is to keep the knee and leg moving. If you try to rest it too much it will stiffen and swell up.' Steve slid off the counter and lowered his weight back onto the knee. It was not quite as painful but stinging like crazy. He thanked Tom profusely as he made his way to the shop door.

'Oh we old timers do occasionally have our uses,' Tom said with a wry smile and a wink. Friday finally arrived and although his knee was still painful he continued flexing it and found the stiffness had eased quite a lot. He silently thanked Tom for all his efforts. Steve was nervous, excited, and totally distracted at school. During the lunch break the team met in the playground and all admitted to having similar feelings. The afternoon dragged slowly by, but when the final bell rang there was a mad, tumbling exodus from the school building.

Spectators were turning up in droves. With just ten minutes to go till kick-off they already lined the perimeter three and four deep, with many more arriving. They were noisy and seriously partisan, each set of supporters trying to outdo the other with their loud chanting and humorous comments. The atmosphere was almost carnival, but for the players the 'butterflies in the stomach' feeling was universal. Steve kept trotting up and down the touchline flexing his knee and keeping on the move.

A sharp blast of the referee's whistle brought the captains to the middle, accompanied by a tremendous roar from the crowd, which by now had swelled to several hundred. From the start Hardy Street played well and took the lead after only six minutes when, under pressure, a Gunton defender sliced the ball into his own net as he attempted a clearance. Playing wide on the right Steve had not seen much of the action, most of it taking place up and down the middle of the pitch. On the few occasions he had been involved he'd cleverly laid the ball off with a first time pass, avoiding physical contact as much as possible. This worked well until just before halftime when the ball was passed to him very hard, bouncing up off the pitch making it difficult to control. The opposing full-back was in on him like a ton of bricks, dumping him unceremoniously on the cinders as he won the ball. Ignoring the loud shouts of `FOUL' from the crowd the referee waved play on, leaving Steve to slowly pick himself up. His shoulder and knee were really hurting now and he was glad when moments later the interval was signalled. During the break with their confidence high, the Hardy Street boys decided to make use of Tom's know-how once more and try for another early goal in the second half.

The plan worked out fine. Immediately after the restart their advantage was doubled by a wonderful goal from Tony Cowans, and this time it was no fluke. Winning the ball inside the centre-circle, he swerved past two Gunton defenders before hitting a glorious shot that left the keeper clutching at thin air. The Hardy Street supporters went wild with delight as the players rushed to congratulate Tony for his magnificent solo effort.

However, the joy turned distinctly sour during the next ten minutes as the Gunton boys battled hard to get back into the game - and they did. First, a trip on Chris Reilly was judged to have been inside the penalty area and they scored from the spot-kick. Then a shot that Jack Wilkes had well covered was deflected beyond his reach by one of his own defenders. All the credit was due to the Gunton players for not giving up and they deserved their piece of luck.

With only minutes to go the roars from the supporters were thundering around the terraced streets as they tried to lift their respective teams for one final effort. The earlier confidence of the Hardy Street team was now replaced by tense desperate defending. The Gunton boys were riding their luck and pushing forward in a last ditch attempt to snatch a winner. The ball was bouncing around the Hardy Street goal mouth like a ping-pong ball. There were shots, blocks and goal line clearances by the second. Suddenly a hard hit shot by Chris Reilly looked to be a winner but it struck Jack Wilkes' left-hand post and rebounded well clear of the congested goal mouth towards Steve. Quickly collecting the ball, he glanced up, realizing there was nothing but open pitch between him and the opposing goalkeeper and began running with it as fast as he could manage. Steve's injuries had taken away a lot of his pace and his knee had begun to throb painfully, but gritting his teeth, he forced himself on. Caught out by the rebound the Gunton players were now streaming back to defend. The full-back who had dumped Steve earlier, was faster than most and made directly for the Hardy Street captain, rapidly shortening the gap between them with each stride. Steve knew his lack of speed would prevent him getting close enough to shoot at goal before the defender was upon him, but a quick glance to his left showed Jimmy Sellers racing up the middle of the pitch, his little legs going like pistons, outpacing the opposing players. If he could keep going for another few yards and square the ball to Jimmy, he would surely score. Now the full-back was level with him and about to make his tackle. It had to be now or the chance would be lost. Steeling himself for the inevitable collision, Steve agonisingly stretched his limbs for the final stride before hooking the ball across into the path of his team-mate. In the same instant, his pursuer tackled him hard. They crashed onto the rough cinders, wincing with pain as they slid and rolled along the pitch in a haze of grey dust.

Because they had fallen, neither had seen Jimmy Sellers collect Steve's pass and ghost past the centre-half on his left side, before rifling an unstoppable shot beyond the groping hands of the Gunton keeper. A deafening roar from the crowd confirmed the outcome as the final whistle sounded. The Hardy Street lads hugged each other with sheer joy. Steve hobbled over to join in the celebrations, and although Jimmy was the centre of attention, he was the first to shake his skipper's hand and thank him for making it possible.

For all the players and supporters the next hour was filled with contrasting emotions; there were winners and losers, joy and disappointment, and neutrals who had just enjoyed a fine match. When the presentation of the trophy and medals was made there was genuine well - deserved applause. It was a very proud Steve Bayliss who received the cup from the newspaper's sports editor. After receiving their medals and posing for photographs, the trophy was held aloft by each player in turn, accompanied by rousing cheers from the crowd.

People began to disperse into the labyrinth of streets surrounding the arena. Darkness descended and the street gas lamps had popped into life one by one, their subdued yellowish light reflecting off the nearby dwellings. With the odd shout of

'We've won the cup' still echoing around the houses, the Hardy Street team ambled back in a loose group to their respective homes. Two or three were looking at their medals while others were admiring the silver cup, knowing that their team's name would shortly be engraved on it forever.

Mr Bayliss and Tom Barber had stopped at the end of Hardy Street and as each of the boys reached the corner they added their congratulations. Tom gripped Steve's hand firmly, an expression of admiration on his face.

STOP, FINISHED

'That was a fine match you lads played out there tonight and your part in it was something special son - something very special indeed.' His lined features cracked into a broad smile as he placed his arm on Steve's shoulder.

'One of those little moments of truth arrived tonight young lad, didn't it? You passed with flying colours as far as I'm concerned. I'll remember it son, just make sure you do.' He squeezed the youngster's hand once more, then turned and limped back up the street to his shop.

In spite of the aches and pains, Steve was up early the following morning. His mother, herself an early riser, was surprised to see him emerge from the cupboard under the stairs with a large cardboard box, into which he placed a hand brush, dustpan and small bucket, then, unlocking the front door, he disappeared without saying a word. On his return an hour later his mother asked what he was up to. The reply was quite casual.

'Oh it's just something the lads in the team decided upon last night.'

'I see,' she said, but in truth was none the wiser.

Returning from the newsagents with his daily paper, Mr Bayliss noticed a large group of people gathered outside Tom Barber's shop window, with others rapidly joining them. He walked across the street, and on drawing closer became fully aware as to what was capturing their interest. The window had been cleaned and in the centre, set upon a covering of dark blue velvet material, which looked suspiciously like a table cloth that had once seen service in the Bayliss household, stood the brightly polished Seven-a-side trophy. Surrounding it were the medals of each of the players, and the whole ensemble bedecked with blue and white ribbons and rosettes. The contrast with the old faded adverts for shoe polish and laces that had once adorned the dusty window was truly amazing. Little wonder it had caught everyone's attention. Stepping around the knot of window gazers he met Tom who was standing in the open shop doorway, his face beaming.

'Isn't it wonderful?' Tom said.

'Your Steve and the rest of the lads were over here first thing this morning asking if they could set this up. What do you think about that?'

'It's a lovely gesture on their part. Perhaps the young locals are not quite as bad as they sometimes appear,' replied Mr Bayliss. Tom agreed, before retreating into the shop, his eyes slightly moist.

Reaching his own front door, Mr Bayliss glanced back to where the people were still clustered around the shop window and felt proud of what Steve and his pals had done.

He also realized that seeing the cup and the medals must have stirred up a few heartbreaking memories for Tom. In a small way perhaps the youngsters of Hardy Street had unknowingly bridged the years by their gesture to the old footballer and redressed the balance a little, for the medal that Tom had played so hard to win but through a cruel twist of fate had never received.

Benny's Superior Guesthouse
- Jack Andrews -

I t was an imposing looking house, built in Victorian style, with a large brass-knobbed front door, great bay windows on both sides and white stone carvings set in the red bricks above. Located in a rather salubrious area of the city it stood apart from the surrounding buildings which housed light engineering works, various small garages and one fish and chip shop. It had been purchased, at a knock down price over thirty years ago by one Benjamin Simon Zuckerman who proceeded to refurbish the building throughout. A large brass plate, adjacent to the bell-push on the front door, was beautifully engraved with the words Benny's Superior Guest House, although if you enquired of the locals, they would always refer to it as Benny's 'doss house'. His guests were a collection of down and outs, itinerants and those weary to the point of exhaustion. They were charged a minimal sum in return for a hot meal and a bed for the night.

Benny was a big hearted man of Jewish parentage who wasn't at all religious and always considered himself to be a lost cause as far as his synagogue was concerned. However, his more acceptable feature lay in his benevolence; he cared for people, especially those who were past caring about themselves, whatever their reasons.

Originally from Germany, the family had fled from Nazi tyranny in the 1930's and settled in England, bringing with them baby Benjamin and whatever else they could manage, including a hoard of jewellery and gold coins secreted in the false bottom of the baby's pram. His jeweller father, Solomon Zuckerman, was a wise and astute man who had visualised how tough life would be in a foreign country. He knew that money was always going to be the main priority. Many years later, on the demise of his parents, Benny was extremely grateful for his father's wisdom, when he became the sole heir to a fair sized fortune. It had been this money that allowed him to purchase and open his guest house. His father taught him to be conscious of the constant need of help for the lower echelons of society and it had prompted Benny to take this particular path in life.

He was a large, rotund man with wisps of grey hair sprouting from either side of a shiny bald pate, who struggled each day to position his bulk behind the desk in his tiny office. Mr Zuckerman had reached his seventieth birthday and was in contemplative mood musing over whether to celebrate alone at a restaurant, or tour his

establishment and talk to his staff and guests. He decided
on the latter – his staff, guests and the running of the house
were more important.

A heavily accented voice shouted his name from
somewhere along the corridor,

'Mr Zuckerman, Mr Zuckerman, can you come
quickly and have a look at this please, I think it is
important?' It was Janic, his live-in handyman. Irritated at
being disturbed he shouted back:

'Alright, alright keep your shirt on,' then easing himself
from behind the desk, banged his knee on the corner and
swore loudly in German, before waddling off to find him.

A young, post-war refugee from Poland and built like a
mountain, Janic had originally been a temporary guest in
the house, but Benny found his carpentry skills so useful to
call upon that he offered him permanent accommodation at
a meagre rent. They got on reasonably well, but Benny
found it difficult to talk with the man. Janic kept himself to
himself saying little as he went about his work each day.
The only occasion that Benny could recall Janic starting a
conversation was the day he brought a small parcel into his
office and began to unwrap it, saying that this was his prized
possession. His face was animated as he peeled off the final
layer of paper disclosing a German Luger pistol complete
with silencer and an eight round clip of bullets, both
wrapped in an oily cloth. Apparently on his trek from
Eastern Europe he had relieved an Army deserter of the
pistol during a brawl outside a tavern. That was Janic's only
explanation as to how he had come to possess the weapon,
and he never spoke of it to his boss again.

Benny eventually found him in the huge cellar beneath
the building, where he was digging up the flagstones in an
attempt to discover the source of a persistent damp

problem. A foul, dank, earthy smell assailed Benny's nostrils as the handyman lifted another of the three foot by two foot stone slabs and manhandled it aside.

'I think this is the worst part of it,' Janic said.

'Worst or otherwise it bloody stinks, so keep digging. Let me know at once if you find anything. It could be the council's water main, it runs parallel to that wall and if it's their fault they can foot the bill.' His labourer grunted an acknowledgement and continued with his task. Benny retreated up the wooden staircase away from the clammy cellar and on reaching the lobby used a large white handkerchief to clear his nose of the stench. He was about to pass the entrance to the dining room when he heard a voice bellowing inside.

'What the bloody hell do you think you're doing, you disgusting pig?' Benny recognised the voice as Bella's, the well endowed female who ran the catering, like a sergeant-major. He looked around the door.

'What's all the commotion about now?' He had heard her blast off at guests many times before. She pointed an accusing finger at the dishevelled looking man hunched over one of the wooden trestle tables.

'It's that mongrel there, putting his fag out in one of my tea mugs.' With hands on hips, she stood behind the serving counter in belligerent pose and muttered: 'Dirty, filthy habit,' before advancing on the offender, who rapidly exited the room. Once a kitchen hand in various sleazy downtown hotels, Bella had now adopted the self-appointed title of chef. She had also spent a six month spell in the kitchen of an H M Prison's establishment in London, but her redeeming feature was that she could always be relied upon to conjure-up a reasonably good meal from limited supplies. The ever tolerant Benny was wise enough to allow Isabella Bellini a great deal of leeway, for in spite of her fierce Latin temperament, she ran a tight ship and that suited him fine. There were other reasons he persevered with Bella, she did all his laundry - and he fancied her.

The drone of bored voices in the council office ceased as Mr. George Ellison, the chairman of the city council's planning committee, pointed to Patrick Riordan.

'Councillor Riordan, would you like to put forward your proposals for the redevelopment of the Commercial Road / Pitt Street area? I know your architect, Mr. Baines, has drawn up detailed plans for the scheme, perhaps you would explain to the committee exactly what it all entails.'

Riordan rose from his seat and confidently strutted across the floor to where a huge street plan was pinned across two boards, set upon easels.

For twenty minutes he spoke about his vision for the future of this large area of the city. The scheme included a completely new estate to house over four thousand people, a shopping mall, community centre, cinema, a large children's play area and all the normal communal facilities. He put his case well. The committee members were impressed, even though they were all aware that Riordan would almost certainly be granted the contract to build the project. Bringing his presentation to a close he said that commencement of building operations would be subject to several businesses in the area having to be removed and compensated, but he did not see that as a problem, he had dealt with this sort of situation many times. One of the businesses referred to was Benny's guest house.

The Riordan Construction Company had been started by Patrick and his father Sean, in the east end of London immediately after the Second World War, when the rebuilding of bombed cities was a priority. On the death of his father, Patrick took control and expanded the company to its present size. A small empire with branches all over the land. Never a tactful man, he operated on the premise of what he couldn't achieve by discussion he could by intimidation and, if necessary, blackmail. Heavily built, with hands like grappling hooks and his neck the girth of a small tree, he had frightened many who had initially opposed him, then completed the deals with offers they couldn't refuse. Although Benny was unaware of it, he was Riordan's next target.

The sleek black, chauffer driven Daimler-Benz silently rolled to a stop alongside the kerb. Riordan stepped from the vehicle and told the driver:

'I'll phone you when I need to return.' Daisy, one of Benny's employees, answered the repeated ringing of the doorbell and directed him to the tiny office, before running off to look for her boss, who she found in the kitchen talking to Bella.

'There's a man in the office waiting to see you Mr Zuckerman, he arrived in a big flash car.'

'What's his name? Benny enquired. A blank expression on Daisy's face told him she hadn't bothered to ask, so he hurried through the lobby to meet his visitor. Arriving in the office doorway, a shiver of apprehension zipped down his spine. He recognised his caller and already knew of his reputation.

'Ah, Mr Zuckerman, my name is Patrick Riordan, I'm a councillor on the city's planning committee and I wish to discuss the rebuilding programme for this area, which of course involves these premises. I've been given the authority to offer you a large amount of money to enable you to consider relocation. Would you like to know how much you would be offered?' Still standing in the entrance, Benny bristled, but controlled his anger.

'Price is not an option as I've no desire to move from here whatsoever. However, if you could include the building of a new guest house in your plans and allow me to run it, I might just be interested.' Riordan's neck reddened as he tried to suppress his annoyance.

'Don't be too hasty Zuckerman, there is always room for negotiation of course.' His tone of voice had suddenly changed. It was icy. Benny brought the brief meeting to a close by stepping back into the lobby and opening the front door, while repeating his earlier statement. As Riordan moved toward the proffered exit, Bella, walking through the lobby with Janic, stopped in her tracks and immediately turned away. When the door closed, she buttonholed Benny.

'What's that creep doing here, Mr Zuckerman?' Benny could see real hatred in her face.

'I didn't realise you knew him.' Bella's face flushed as she replied:

'Oh I've come across him before, when I worked in London.' Benny, still trembling a little from his confrontation with Riordan, sat down and told Bella exactly what had taken place. As he finished relating what had ensued, Janic silently appeared in the doorway and confirmed that the damp in the cellar was definitely due to the leaking water-main. Benny wondered whether his handyman had heard what he had been telling Bella.

Within the hour, a second visitor arrived at the house. George Gillmott, the owner of the largest of the car repair shops on the Commercial Road, stood in the office, his face as white as a sheet; it was obvious he had been badly shaken. Spluttering his words, he told of a visit by Riordan, who had quite openly threatened to wreck his business if he didn't accept the offer made to him. Calming his neighbour down with a large helping of whisky, Benny suggested that they should ask all the others who had premises on the road whether Riordan had called upon them. Bella, still present when George related his frightening tale, volunteered to help and they set out to make their enquiries around the locality. The result was alarming. Riordan had visited the owners of eight other businesses and directly threatened five of them. The remainder had not argued. Drastic measures needed to be taken and a meeting was quickly arranged for those interested in making a stand. Riordan had told the undecided owners he would be back later that evening, to help them make up their minds.

Returning from their inquiries, Mr Zuckerman joined Bella in the dining room for a cup of tea and when seated, quietly said:

'What did you mean, Bella, when you mentioned you knew Riordan in London?'

'Oh, I just came into contact with him a few times.' She shied away from a more detailed answer, but he was very persistent and in the end Bella disclosed everything.

'As you can guess, with my background I would never have been 'deb'of the year, but at nineteen years old I was considered to be quite a beauty. Fashion modelling and cosmetics was my thing and I was doing quite well until that sleazebag Riordan and his wife Fiona clapped eyes on me. They wanted someone to run their high-class escort agency. And made me a very good offer along with a big salary. I couldn't really refuse – yes, Patrick was very persuasive even then. It was alright in the beginning, but then Riordan wanted his perks and assumed his perks included me. When I refused he got nasty and threatened to rearrange my face, in fact I still carry some of the scars he treated me to. In the end I scarpered, but swore I'd get him back one day. From that point on it was all downhill. Thieving, shoplifting, credit card fraud and inevitably I ended up on the game, which eventually booked me a six month stay in Holloway.' Benny listened to her saga without interruption, then gently placing his hand on her shoulder, whispered:

'In my eyes you're still a beauty, and somehow we'll fix Riordan's wagon.'

Bella, her eyes moist, did not respond to his tenderness and left quickly, saying she had somewhere to go. She didn't normally succumb to tears so easily. Dashing upstairs with her cheeks still wet, Bella made directly for Janic's room. The pair had been lovers for some time without most of the staff, including Benny, being aware. Once in his room she broke down completely, lying face down on his bed in floods of tears, snuffling out all that she had just told Benny about her past. Although the details came as a surprise to Janic, it didn't prevent him from putting his huge arms about her in a gesture of comfort. He loved Bella. She felt warm and secure when they were together, and her everyday brash persona was discarded.

Detective Chief Inspector Dave Reynolds had just turned on his television to watch 'Match of the Day', when his bleeper sounded. Before he answered, he just knew he was not going to be watching any football that evening – and he was right. Detective Sergeant Barry Chilvers informed him that a man's body had been discovered in an abandoned house at the rear of the Commercial Road workshops. Reynolds told him he was on his way.

There were very few street lights in the area and the crime scene could only be reached by struggling over broken brickwork and debris of old, partly demolished houses. By the time the Chief Inspector arrived, the Scenes of Crime Officers had finished photographing and recording the necessary details, but at Reynolds' request they left their portable lighting units at the scene.

The body was lying face down in a partly sheltered corner of a wrecked dwelling, a corner that stank of urine, vomit and putrid damp. Scattered around it were discarded pizza cartons, broken beer bottles, cans, cardboard boxes and greasy chip wrappings, but the point that caught Reynolds attention was the quality of the man's overcoat and suit. They were expensive. Within moments the on-call pathologist arrived, wheezing and puffing after manoeuvring his way across the waste ground. It was Dr. Ludwig van Thiegster, known to most of the CID as Luddy. After a brief inspection and commenting that the back of the deceased's head looked like it had been bashed with a brick, he asked Dave to help him turn the body over. Pulling on latex gloves, they rolled the body onto its back and Dave recognised the victim immediately. The only difference from when he had last seen him was that Riordan's face now sported a neatly drilled hole in the middle of his forehead, complete with powder burns. The DCI sarcastically said,

'Whoever did this certainly didn't intend to miss.' Luddy took a closer look at the circular wound.

'Going by the size of the entry hole I suspect it is a 9mm, and it's possible you may find it has exited through the damage at the rear of his skull.' The Chief Inspector was already looking back to where they had rolled the body. It took him fifteen minutes scrabbling about in the debris on the floor before he located it. The bullet was damaged, but still recognizable as a 9mm. He placed it in a small plastic evidence bag saying he would take it to the laboratory as soon as he had finished here; it might just be the clue they needed. He then spoke to the constable who first phoned the crime in to his station.

'Who actually found the body?'

'He's outside sir, shakin' like a leaf. His name's Charlie Moon.'

'Bring him in here please.' Seconds later, accompanied by a loud muttering about how he had been scared to death, Charlie was ushered in. The Chief Inspector told the trembling wreck of a man to be quiet and only speak when asked a question. The sternness in Reynolds' voice had the desired effect. He shut up.

'How did you come to discover the body, and why were you here at all?' Charlie began to stutter, until the DCI gripped his arm and told him to take his time.

'I didn't have enough money to go to Benny's around the corner so I found some old cardboard boxes and decided to kip in ere'. That's when I fell over him and it scared the shit out of me an' I ran out as fast as I could. Your young copper will back me up, he saw me running down the road an' he stopped me, an' I went back with him, an' I showed him.'

'Did you see anyone else when you first got here?' Charlie hesitated before answering.

'No, there wasn't nobody about, I didn't see anyone.'

'Did you take anything from the pockets of the deceased?'

'Not bloody likely, I couldn't get out of ere' fast enough.'

'When you were making your way here with your cardboard boxes did you hear anything, a shot, or a loud bang?'

'I told yer', I didn't see or 'ear anything.' The pathologist quietly motioned to the DCI that he had something to tell him, and they moved outside.

'I took the liberty of checking our late friend's pockets while I was dealing with him and discovered a great bundle of fifty pound notes. There must be several thousands of pounds at least, so I think you can discard robbery as the motive. Another thing is the scuffing on the heels of his shoes, it looks as though he was killed somewhere else then dragged inside here.'

'Thanks Luddy, I'll just send this Charlie Moon character to headquarters where I can question him properly.' He told the constable who had found him to take Charlie back to the station and give him some tea, or possibly a hot meal.

Rejoining Luddy, they started to make a more in-depth examination of the scene. Reynolds took another look at the wound at the back of Riordan's head. There was not enough blood on the floor to suggest he had been struck where he had been found. He voiced his thoughts to the pathologist. Luddy nodded in agreement, then said:

'I know its early days Dave, but for what it's worth I believe this character was dead before the shooting took place. Whoever smashed that brick into his head did so with so much force that I cannot see how anyone could survive such a blow.' Reynolds listened to Luddy's comments then answered:

'That more or less bears out the lack of blood where we found him.' The DCI immediately ordered several of the uniformed constables to cordon off a much greater area than had already been done. He wanted it extended to the rear of all the premises that fronted on to the Commercial Road. Turning again to Dr.Thiegster he said:

'This needs to be done in daylight. It will have to be an inch by inch search, with plenty of uniforms; looking for a blood trail over ground like this is akin to looking for a needle in the proverbial haystack.' Leaving the site, Reynolds made his way back over the rough ground, heading for the police station to talk again with Charlie Moon. On the journey he mused over the outline and details of the case so far. Something didn't add up he thought. Why, after bashing the victim's head in would someone go to the trouble of dragging him inside a derelict house just to put a bullet in his skull at close range? There was some very deep seated anger in this murder.

Charlie Moon didn't add anything further to what he had already said, so Reynolds released him, with a warning to stay close to the area. With hands outstretched, palms upwards, Charlie said that he wasn't going anywhere; his gesture also denoting he was skint. The DCI heaved a huge sigh and rolled his eyes heavenwards as he dug into his pocket and passed Charlie a five pound note, with a suggestion that he try Benny's establishment if he wanted a good night's kip.

Early the following morning, in slanting icy rain, a team of detectives descended on the premises in Commercial Road, to interview all the occupants. During the questioning of George Gillmott they discovered that Riordan had returned later that evening, repeating his threats to George and two other owners, Jim Sale and Harry Jackson. He also visited Benny's guest house around ten-o-clock but was again met with the angry proprietor's refusal to accept his offer.

At the same time, to the rear of the buildings, uniformed police were finger-tip searching the waste ground in an attempt to pinpoint where the attack on the victim took place. Four hours of cold, wet, painstaking graft had taken place before a shout went up that something had been found. DS Barry Chilvers, as senior co-ordinator, moved quickly to where a small group of uniforms' were gathered, looking at something on the ground close to an old battered dustbin. Pulling on latex gloves, he approached them and shouted:

'What yer got?'

'Don't really know Serg', but it could be what you're looking for.'

DS Chilvers went ballistic when he saw the broken brick, with blood and hair attached lying uncovered in the heavy rain.

'Jesus Christ, don't they teach you blokes anything in plod school about preserving evidence?' He quickly produced a large plastic evidence bag from his pocket and with deft touches managed to manoeuvre the two pieces of the brick inside, before inserting it into an even larger brown paper container. The uniforms' stood around watching him as he completed the retrieval, which infuriated him even more and he shouted again:

'Don't just stand around; get on with it, there might be more. One of you ring headquarters and get the SOCO back here. Mark the position with a stick or something, it's got to be recorded.' The expressions on the faces of the remaining coppers' turned sullen, accompanied by murmurings of discontent, a situation that often existed between the uniform branch and CID. The only other item to be found during the remainder of the search was a size five black shoe with a silver, butterfly shaped buckle. The shoe, to fit a right foot, was reasonably new but had been very badly scuffed and was now reduced to a soggy pulp, having absorbed so much of the torrential rain.

The Commercial Road was a hive of activity early the next day when three port-a-cabins were set down in a neat row parallel to the pavement. Two would serve as the Murder HQ and the third would house a make-shift canteen. Another team of detectives set about the task of re-interviewing everyone who had been in, or near the vicinity on the night of the murder. They again questioned in depth, all the owners and staff of the various businesses, as well as the guests at Benny's. The only further thing of note that surfaced was when Mrs Sally Jardine, who owned the chip shop, mentioned what had happened after she closed her shop just after ten-fifteen that night. Switching off all the fryers and lights, she had gone outside in the back area to have a smoke before locking up and setting off home. She hadn't heard any shots or loud reports, but thought she had heard a woman's voice followed by scraping sounds, as if someone was stumbling across the brick debris on the waste land at the rear. This piece of information was limited in itself, but valuable as regards the time element. When asked why she hadn't volunteered this information before, she said she thought it might have been someone staggering back home after a boozy night out and wasn't important. The DCI had put a stop on all the rubbish bins and skips in the area being collected and had them searched thoroughly for anything that might shed some light on the murder, but nothing of use was found. The searching and questioning continued for days but no further evidence came to the surface.

A slightly frustrated Dave Reynolds returned to Benny's house and carefully went through the statements made by the staff and guests and under further questioning discovered the liaison that existed between Bella and Janic, an item that had not come to his attention before. He began to question them further.

'When you returned from seeing all the other owners where did you go and did anyone see you?' Without meeting Reynolds' gaze, Bella said:

'I was talking with Benny, then I went up to Janic's room, we stayed there all night he can vouch for me.' Janic nodded his head in agreement.

'I understand you knew Riordan before coming here, is that right?' Reynolds' cold blue eyes never shifted from Bella's face as he put the question to her. Bella realised there was no sense in trying to deny it. She knew after serving time in Holloway he would have full details of her background. She grudgingly gave a shortened version of the details, but still avoided the DCI's gaze.

'What size shoes do you wear, Miss Bellini?' Her head came up instantly and her face flushed as she answered without thinking.

'Size five,' she blurted out.

'That's interesting,' Reynolds said as he produced a clear plastic bag containing the shoe found on the waste ground.

'Is this yours by any chance?' He held the bag up to Bella's eye level to see if there was any reaction, but there was none. She had regained her composure as she stared at the bag, then answered with a defiant,

'No. I wouldn't wear rubbish like that anyway.' The DCI turned his attention to Janic.

'Do you and Bella have any plans for the future?' The question was unexpected but the answer was immediate.

'We are going to get married. We shall go back to Poland to work on my uncle's farm in Niepolomice. It is near Krakow.'

'Please accept my congratulations, perhaps you'll invite me to the wedding.'

'If you like.' Bella answered sarcastically. Reynolds realised there was nothing more to be gained from either of them and brought the interview to a close by advising that he would probably want to talk to them again. The staff grapevine eventually conveyed to Benny the situation between Bella and Janic and their proposed marriage. He was saddened, not only because he would lose them, but because of his affection for Bella. It was probably at this low point that he decided to look to his retirement, but not before he had extracted a promise from the Council's Planning Committee. He requested that if his relocation compensation was returned to their budget, would they build a new night-shelter within the development. After several months, the committee agreed to this, which made Benny a much happier man.

There were no further clues or information about the murder for several weeks and although the case could not be officially closed, its momentum did slow down; but it never left the thoughts of DCI Reynolds even though his workload continually increased. In his mind he was convinced he knew who had carried out the murder, but without concrete proof he couldn't progress.

During the demolition and site clearing for the new development, there was one day which temporarily raised the hopes of Reynolds and his team. A digger driver was working the area that had once housed the cellar of the guesthouse. Handling his JCB machine with great skill he charged into the rubble again and again, each time lifting a half-ton of debris high in the air before depositing the load into the back of a high sided truck. The last action before the morning tea break was almost completed when something caught his eye. A singular object had fallen to the ground from the top of the giant scoop. Turning off the engine he climbed down to investigate. Jim Langley looked to the muddy ground at what appeared to be a section of a metal pipe joint but on closer inspection realised it was something he had seen many times before when serving in the Army during World War Two. Although covered in a brown slime he recognised the familiar shape of a German Luger pistol and, unusually, this one had a silencer attached. His first reaction was to pick it up but then he had second thoughts and called out to his foreman to telephone the police.

DS Barry Chilvers collected the weapon within twenty minutes of receiving the call and took it directly to the laboratory of the firearms department at headquarters. The technicians discovered there were seven live bullets in the magazine and set about thoroughly cleaning and oiling the gun, before making comparison tests with the cartridge found by DCI Reynolds. Forty-eight hours later they were able to confirm that the bullet that had passed through Riordan's skull had been fired from that weapon.

Dave Reynolds was delighted with the news. At home that evening, enjoying his favourite highland malt whisky, he reflected on the events of this particular murder. He was convinced of three things. His first point was that the killer, or killers, knew Riordan personally. The next point, which he couldn't really pin down, was the reason for the victim to be dragged into the derelict building before shooting him, when it was almost a certainty that Riordan was either dead or very close to death from the impact of the blow with the brick. His last point was something he had voiced to himself when still at the crime scene, that whoever fired the single bullet into Riordan's head must have been seething with anger to have committed such an act. Dave had his strong suspicions as to who had carried out the murder but was not in a position to close the case or make an arrest because of the lack of irrefutable evidence.

The days and weeks stretched into months without any conclusion and Riordan's murder eventually became a statistic on the unsolved pile, from where it would inevitably end up in the cold cases section. The local newspapers seldom printed anything on the murder now, except for an occasional 'who did it' article. It was no longer considered newsworthy. During this period Benny retired, as he said he would, to live in a luxury flat in the south of the city and Janic and Bella married in the local Registry Office, before moving to his uncle's farm in Poland. George Gillmott, who had been one of the stronger suspects because of his angry reaction to the event, had opened another business with the relocation grant the council had paid and was prospering in another town. Three and a half years on, the estate and community project was completed and became a thriving success; it also won a national award for the architect, Mr. Ronald Baines.

★ ★ ★

Bella sang quietly to herself as she pegged out the days' washing on the clothes-line erected down the side of her small vegetable garden. The sun was fierce as it beat down from the azure blue sky, with the odd white clouds appearing almost as intruders. As she sang, she was in thoughtful mood, reflecting on her good fortune since meeting Janic. Looking across the valley at the endless acres of green fields and conifers, dissected only by the wide, glistening River Vistula, she crossed herself as she thanked God for his blessings over the last few years. She thought of

Janic working hard in the fields for his uncle Igor, she thought of the lovely cottage they had been given to live in, but most of all she thought of her beautiful daughter Genovieve who was four years old today. Yes, she had a lot to thank God for.

Earlier that day Bella had baked a large chocolate birthday cake which now stood on the table by the opened latticed windows. She was about to complete the decorations when Genovieve ran into the kitchen and said:

'Because it's my birthday Mummy, can I play dressing-up and use your lipstick and make-up. Please Mummy – please?' Bella would never willingly disappoint her daughter and immediately said:

'Of course you can darling. All the old clothes are in the shed at the end of the garden and when you use my lipstick please don't make a mess on the dressing table.' Almost before she had said it, Genovieve, with her long corn coloured hair flying behind her was through the door and on her way to her mother's bedroom.

Bella had started preparing for the party when her daughter reappeared in the kitchen doorway, her face made up so well that it almost looked as if it had been applied by an expert. Her small, tanned features crowned by beautiful blonde tresses didn't need much artificial enhancement, just a little of the right shade of lipstick was perfect and she had chosen the right colour. Bella didn't utter a word. She just gazed and admired her child's beauty and visualised how she would look in the coming years.

'Does it look alright Mummy, have I done it right?'

'It couldn't be better Geno, its perfect.'

'Can I look for some dresses now then?'

'Yes darling, you know where they are.' The little girl skipped her way down the garden and spent the next half hour rummaging among large cardboard boxes and old suitcases, trying on several dresses, hats and shoes. It was great fun.

Janic arrived home from work and Bella was about to call Geno to get ready for her party when she walked through the kitchen door carrying an old box. She looked a picture, dressed in one of Bella's old dresses, pulled up around her waist to stop her tripping. Her father joked about how she looked just like her mother used to.

'I've had a lovely time in the shed trying on lots of clothes, but I can't find any nice shoes.' Genovieve placed the box on the table and as she started to remove the contents, Janic immediately glanced at Bella, their expressions changed from happiness to sheer horror, as she said.

'The shoe I did like was this one, with the beautiful silver butterfly buckle. Do you know where the other one is, Mummy?'

Evelyn Danbury

Evelyn Danbury lives in North Norfolk and is retired. She
has worked in sales, marketing and publicity/PR for mass
market publishers, with high profile best selling authors.
More recently she was Fundraiser/PR for a local charity.
Her interests include, gardening, creative writing and
Norfolk life.

Evelyn Danbury

Time Piece
- Evelyn Danbury -

S he would have to move the body. She was absolutely certain about that. She had got up very early and had wandered through the quiet house. It had been light for some time but the sunshine of the dawn had given way to a dull cold bleak morning. As she sipped her tea she heard all the clocks of the house, Josiah's collection, chiming, or in the case of the earliest ones, ringing in salute of eight o'clock. How she hated the clocks! Clocks were an obsession of Josiah's even before their marriage. Clocks and guns of course. When the carillons finally subsided she was able to collect her thoughts. Josiah was a large man by any standards and in death of course he had not lost any of his bulk. In fact he seemed bulkier than ever, sprawled out on the rug like that. He was much too heavy to move but move him she knew she must. He contributed nothing to the ambience of the sitting room and would be decidedly in her way.

She abandoned her short vigil and went to the kitchen in search of more tea and toast. On the way she kicked the door of the gun cupboard shut, making a mental note that the latch should really be fixed. In between the crashing and crunching noises in her head a plan formulated itself. She would drag him into the conservatory and leave him behind the sofa. He could stay on the hearthrug for the time being. No one would see. There was no one to see. No one to go in. Then later she would have to bury him. Yes that was it! In the garden. Near where the dogs were buried, under the trees. He'd like that. Yes! that's what she'd do then.

Out of habit, she consulted her diary. Hair appointment in Westbury. She would cancel. Then the heading 'London' for the week and just blank spaces. She felt like a blank space in someone else's diary. Wife of Josiah , mother of his two children, both grown up and long gone. James to the army and Sarah to London. And she was left behind, stalwart of the Church Flower Group, Women's Institute and Village Life. Wife and shadowy figure behind Josiah's success as a businessman, pillar of the community and inveterate charity committee man. All those dreary receptions, interminable speeches, boring people. Is it any wonder she had despatched him last night? Not a bad shot considering she'd never been one for guns, in fact .....

Her reverie was interrupted by the familiar noise of the back door being flung open and then crashing against the kitchen wall. Josiah himself erupted breezily into the room, muddy labradors at his heels.

"Daphers, don't just sit there looking as if you've seen a ghost! Got to get all prettied up for the big day. The kids'll be here soon. Be like going on a family holiday all over again! Hotel's all booked, you know the Royal Horseguards, the one you like, rooms overlooking the river and you can hear Big Ben, and then we'll all go out to supper bit of a celebration eh? Not everyday we all go off to the Palace for the OBE is it?" and then more gruffly: "Just as much yours darling as it is mine you know." Then regaining control, he urged, "Come on old bones chop! chop! Get ready and I'll run you over to, er, what's her name er, Madame Pompoms and for heaven's sake stop playing with that bloody gun!"

The Lighthouse
- Evelyn Danbury -

He looked out of the window. The lighthouse. The lighthouse as always standing silently sentinel. Encompassing the cottage and him in its unrelenting, unremitting, rhythmic glare.

He turned and began to close the curtains at the windows, which overlooked the lighthouse itself and the dark brooding menace of the sea beyond. He then closed all the curtains in the room against the gathering dusk and the gathering storm.

In the beginning, when he first came to the island in search of solitude and peace and quiet, he found the lighthouse to be a staunch ally. He had enjoyed the silence, the only hustle and bustle that of flocks of sea birds, waders and geese, darkening the skies in their thousands. And the only sounds those of synchronised wing beats and the discordant chorus of their cries.

The remoteness of the small Scottish isle, its inaccessibility had drawn him as indeed had the lighthouse itself, standing so close to the cottage. But lately he had become troubled by the fact that the lighthouse had its own agenda. He couldn't control it. He felt subject to it, in that he certainly couldn't escape the beam or switch it off. The early comfort that being within the light's range had afforded had gradually been eroded and now he was irritated by it and yet helpless to escape it. Just him and the monstrous white, edifice locked in a one-sided embrace. He tossed more logs on the fire, watched the sparks career wildly up the chimney and placed another unopened bottle of the "amber nectar" on the tray on the small table by his fireside chair. The start of another evening. The gradual death of the fire, the warming, then numbing of the whisky. Oblivion and the awakening to hangover, chill, wretchedness and the slow return to the consciousness of the same situation, the same problems, not eased by flight or solitude or drink. Just the solitude holding them in abeyance, like some perpetual pending tray in a filing system, where they waited for inspection by the probing lighthouse beam. The island was not turning out to be the solution he had hoped for. Perhaps there was not going to be a solution. His eyes strayed, as they habitually did, to the gun cupboard. But for tonight at least he knew he would not stir from the hearth. No, not for tonight.

The lighthouse had stood on the edge of the smooth, white sandy beach for as long as anyone could remember. Over the years the Moraig Bank had claimed its fair share of victims, vessels homeward bound, outward bound rig support boats and even wartime submarines. There was a simple stone memorial nearby, recording the names of the poor souls known to be lost to a watery grave, with a prayer in the Gaelic for all those lost at sea.

Neighbouring islands offered trips to visit the Moraig Lighthouse. Some said it had a siren quality and had lured sailors off course but this was just moonshine. It had originally been manned by a team of two men but their days belonged to the island's history. Now its only human contact was the maintenance crew, which serviced the light at prescribed intervals with cheery disregard for its sombre heritage. The lighthouse was known to the locals as Leonora. Rumour had it that a former Laird had rashly imported a bride from The Borders who was tall and statuesque and aloof and somehow reminiscent of the lighthouse.

He opened his eyes to ice. No frost. No frosted glass. Slowly his brain, numbed by alcohol thawed into consciousness. Frosted glass – so he was in the bathroom. On the floor. Again. Having vomited and passed out. As was his routine. Then the blinding light, searing through the darkness of his brain, bouncing off his eyeballs, leaving pinpricks of coloured lights dancing in the blackness of his skull. He felt hollow, weak and cold. How long had he been here this time? Did it matter? Did he care? Just the same as usual. Another day. This was how he always awoke to another day. This was his life. Life? If you could call it that. He slid himself across to the wash basin and hauled himself up its pedestal, gripping both sides for support. He looked in the mirror above it. He was confronted by a dishevelled, weary, sick looking individual whom he could hardly recognise as his former self. Haunted grey eyes set in a pallor of a face, badly in need of a wash let alone a shave. He ran his hand through the dark matted hair, splashed his face with cold water, scrubbed a toothpaste-less toothbrush round his mouth, spat out forcefully and prepared to turn round. This was tricky. He would have to relinquish the one-handed grip on the wash basin. He let go, turned and the room took flight. Too fast. He reeled and had to wait for the bathroom to right itself. Steadied, he then made for the door. He negotiated this and then the stairs very carefully and thus slowly gained the kitchen. He half-heartedly thought about a swig from a new bottle but found he actually wanted tea to quench his thirst. But was he up to making it? He lumbered clumsily through the familiar motions of this task and then sat with his back to the window, back to the beam to sip it. It made him retch but he persevered. And kept most of the cupful down. He sat there for ages waiting for the beam to sweep the kitchen. Then again and again. Rhythmically and relentlessly. He tried to collect his thoughts, to think but there was the light again. Curtains open, curtains closed, it made no difference. Later he dozed and drifted in and out of fitful sleep.

Once he thought he heard Hamish come and go with the supplies. Hamish was all things to all men on the island. He was the Laird's right hand man, provider of provender from the mainland and the fount of all local knowledge. The island's own Mr Fixit. Hamish had begun to keep an eye out for the sorry occupant of the Laird's cottage at his wife Katrina's behest.

"That poor godforsaken soul," she said, "if ever a body need a helping hand Hamish, it is he." Which Hamish took to mean he was to go and check the cupboards for supplies or lack of them, rectify the situation and to keep an eye on the fuel supply. But he did not stir. And Hamish would not disturb him. He had the keys and sometimes would come in to wind the clocks, check out the boiler or make sure the shutters were secure. To be honest Hamish had at the beginning attempted conversation, but this didn't lead anywhere and he had given up. Katrina packed a basket every day or so with her own bread and scones and Hamish was to leave the pot of broth heating on the range. Only to find it untouched. Sometimes the pot was empty but

Hamish knew that the tenant had thrown the contents down the sink. The truth was he was beyond food. Whisky had become his meat and drink. Hamish was irritated by his wife's concern for the tenant and Katrina was well aware of it. However she reminded herself that she was a McGregor before she was a McLaren and the McGregors at least were good Christian folk, who kept an eye out for the needy. Hamish returned from his trip to the cottage in disgruntled mood.

"What's he doing here anyway, for all the good its doing him? He'll drink himself to death at this rate. Such a ..."

But Katrina settled down to her weaving and reflected that maybe there was a reason for the stranger's presence. And she continued to think about this long after Hamish had stomped around, before going about his island business, the dogs unbidden at his heels.

Later the tenant stirred to rifle through the boxes outside in search of a new case of whisky. He found a case and fumbled to undo it. He grabbed a bottle, went back into the kitchen, opened it, took a good swig and then dozed again, seated at the kitchen table with his head on his arms. He awoke to the beam and knew something was different. He had made a decision. He had had enough! He had had enough! His relationship with the lighthouse had run its course. He could stand it no longer. He knew he must kill the light and then, and only then would he be able to think. The mercilessly incessant rhythm of the light had driven him to this dire remedy. He wrenched open the gun cupboard, grabbed the first gun that fell towards him, kicked the rest back and slammed the cupboard door shut. He then flung open the front door intending to load it on the empty, gale-lashed beach.

Not so.

The beach was no longer empty or quiet. It was thronging unexpectedly with a host of people, mostly islanders, some busy with their boats. There was a rescue helicopter landed away to the left and people, were yelling to make themselves heard above the raging of the winds, the sea and the helicopter's engine. A man in uniform, wearing a yellow fluorescent jacket, the coastguard he presumed, strode authoritatively towards him and the cottage.

He called out: "Good evening sir, we won't be needing that," indicating the gun, "but I've come to ask you if we can commandeer the cottage. We've got survivors from the wrecked ship to process and it's such a filthy night we need to get them sheltered. Your help would be much appreciated," he finished with the kind of manner that was used to being obeyed. The tenant could only nod by way of answer. Not just because of the shock of the situation and the wreck of his plans, but because he was unused to speaking with anyone.

He hadn't spoken with anyone for several weeks, except for Hamish who remained resolutely incurious about the stranger's life and was himself taciturn. His face was wooden. He felt that to speak would split his jaw. Anyway he couldn't think now of what would be appropriate to say in any circumstances and, more precisely, these.

He retreated to the cottage, shoved the gun in the cupboard and made for the kitchen. But the cottage was being taken over by officialdom and goodwill. The kitchen was needed for the supply of hot drinks, if that was OK? He nodded assent and let the human tide of organised compassion and practical help surge past him. He couldn't grasp what had happened. He couldn't summon the resolve to ask. Maybe he didn't care. And he felt helpless and irrelevant in the drama that was unfolding perfectly well without him.

At 22.00 on 17th January 2007 RAF Rothesay received the message about the plight of Drummer Alpha rig, in the Dexter field. The rig had been on tow, and had been caught out by the sudden and severe weather conditions and was now listing badly. A rescue helicopter had already been scrambled to pick up some rig workers. Others had been taken aboard the standby vessel, Blue Merlin.

Flt Lt Giles, the handling Pilot, Rescue 197 was experienced and used to atrocious mission conditions but tonight this was really something else. He flew out to the stricken rig, circled her and made ready for the descent on to the brilliantly lit, steeply angled heli-pad below him. As he was about to make the descent the rig's emergency power failed, and Drummer Alpha was immediately devoured by the greedy darkness. He had no more sight of her, just his inward memory.

The co Pilot said: "We're not going down, not when we can't see?"

Flt Lt Giles affirmed without hesitation: "We're going down!"

The Winchman knew Flt Lt Giles very well. He acknowledged, thinking, no surprises there then! It was a very hairy descent. The most dangerous that the Flt Lt had ever attempted. Although he had only his visual memory, his skill, courage and grim determination to see the job through urged him on. The storm and seas were unprecedented in their ferocity, but there were men down there hanging on for grim death. So there was no doubt in his cool, clear brain and valiant heart.

The last man was stowed safely aboard and it was time for the equally impossible ascent. The lurching angle of the heli-pad was against him, the weather was against him, the darkness was against him. Everything was against him. But he made to lift off. Easy as she goes. They cleared the rig safely but minutes later the control panel lit up like a Christmas tree.

"Gear box!" they said in unison. Then attempting a conversational tone which belied his fear for their safety, Flt Lt Giles continued, "It's not too clever I know, but we're just over Moraig. There's her light. Then the co pilot wondered if he had lost it as he heard him call out to the Winchman. "Let's go see Leonora!"

The damaged helicopter had reported her position and status back to base, advised they would make Moraig lighthouse beach, and requested a relief helicopter to rendezvous there for transfer of all rig personnel and helicopter crew.

The co-Pilot locked his eyes on the control panel as smoke swirled around the cockpit and small pieces of molten metal began to rain down on them from above. The descent was horrific, the noise overwhelming, the juddering vibrations increasing in severity as they plummeted downwards. Yet under the beneficent rhythmic lighthouse beam, vying with the lightning to punctuate the darkness, they managed to land the blazing helicopter on the smooth expanse of the lighthouse beach.

You got to hand it to him, thought the Winchman, boy could that guy fly! as he jumped down on to terra firma. Flt Lt Giles the last to leave breathed sotto voce, "God bless Leonora!" as he too ran for his life up the terrifyingly illuminated beach in the wake of the others.

The tenant had taken refuge in the sitting room. The whole cottage was full of bustling women, under the control of Katrina. He vaguely wondered where all those blankets and rugs and neat piles of clothing had suddenly appeared from. Hamish was outside helping to direct the island volunteers and working like a Trojan. Katrina brought a steaming mug of cocoa to the tenant.

"Drink up now!" she couldn't help saying, thinking how he looked as if he could do with it, the poor wretch. He took the steaming mug from her and stared at the fire someone had miraculously revived and reflected on what had brought him here to Moraig.

He remembered that chance conversation with his neighbour in London. She had just returned from a holiday, more like a retreat, he had thought at the time, from some obscure Scottish island,

"If ever you want to get away, need real peace and quiet, somewhere to think, then Moraig is the place and you just ask to rent the Laird's cottage and it's perfect! Slap bang next to the most wonderful lighthouse!" She handed him a card with the number and details and he passed it to Jenny his wife, who dutifully filed it in the top drawer of her bureau.

In the aftermath of his wife's death the island came back inexplicably to haunt him. Jenny had been killed instantly. Car crash. That was a shock in itself, but it was excruciating to learn that the driver, who had survived with a few bumps and bruises, was in fact her lover. The sad fact was that Jenny had already left him. He found the obligatory note in the time-honoured place on the mantelpiece and had hardly had time to assimilate it when that knock, that no nonsense bad news kind of knock, reverberated through the house. He half hoped that Jenny would be standing there. A change of heart. No. It was a uniformed constable whose solemn demeanour betrayed the gravity of the news he was about to impart.

Life after that had descended rapidly into chaos. He couldn't think, couldn't cope, couldn't concentrate. He made a hell of a mess of things at work. Lost the company a deal of money. And regretful as the company was, the time came when they had to part. A sympathetic meeting, a carefully composed letter with a handwritten note from the elderly father figure on the board saying if ever there was anything he could do personally and wishing him godspeed.

In truth he was relieved that someone had made some kind of decision. Had taken control. He couldn't. That was for sure. The severance pay was not ungenerous. The drinking took on a deeper commitment and it was then that the Scottish island hove into his clouded brain. And it kept coming. Insisting even. Almost a kind of summons. Inexplicably he found himself making his way there. Nothing to stay for in London. No chance of a job. He couldn't work. He didn't actually want to work at the moment anyway. The house would keep. He couldn't be bothered with the hassle of airports and so took the train northward. He enjoyed for a brief moment the memory of childhood holidays over the border, when his father would go off to join a shooting party with friends and he and his mother would have a more child friendly Scottish holiday by the sea. It would be some years before he would learn how to handle a hunting rifle and develop a passion for guns. He looked out seaward at Berwick and then savoured the Scottish countryside. On the island he found the cottage as promised in the lea of the lighthouse. And then the solitude. Too much solitude. The protection and comfort of the light and then its dominance. The dominance of the light and the dominance of the drinking. The isolation not helping and the drunken ritual taking a grim hold of him, a descent into a sort of demi-monde of hallucination, memories and bitterness. Guilt, regret and sheer bloody pain. Had he driven her away to her lover? Driven her away to her death as it happened. So it was his fault? And for him what was there? No job. No identity. No occupation. No reason to carry on. No wife, no children, no family just a house, an empty house full of memories, a car and the hangovers. Oh Christ!

Katrina was back at his side

"We're giving everyone hot broth and bread and cheese. Now will you take some? We're so grateful for the kitchen and the use of the cottage. We could be doing nothing of this without you", she almost crooned, sensing that this was one way to reach him.

Somehow gradually heartened, perhaps by the presence of purposeful people in the cottage, he sampled the broth and found that he could drink it. He finished the broth and then ate all the bread and cheese. Katrina then brought him a slice of her raspberry tart, but he had fallen asleep and so she let him be. She quietly ushered the last of the helpers from the house when they had all done all they could for the folk. She stayed to tidy up and to clean the kitchen at least to "new pin" standard, resolving to come back as soon as she possibly could to set the whole cottage to rights. She then left, but not until she had looked in again on the tenant, still sleeping like a bairn. She looked over toward the lighthouse and the mainland beyond, aware that her daughter, working in the hospital, would be in for a very busy night.

He awoke with a start and found he was curious to know what was happening on the beach and was surprised to find that he had the energy to pursue his curiosity. He grabbed his jacket and flung it on. He noticed gloves, driving gauntlets on the hall table. He hadn't seen them before and he didn't need them now.

He opened the door, and walked down the path. A blazing helicopter was on the beach with the passengers and crew racing away from it up the beach. Then a rumble and a blast. He heard the crump and saw more flames erupting. He could see the one of the Pilots caught by the blast lying on the beach presumably unconscious, and started to move towards him.

Suddenly he was running, then racing across the beach, cursing the lighthouse for not shedding more of its light on his path. The heat was intense and the smoke thick and acrid. He was aware that there might be a further explosion at any moment but despite that, and because of that, ran on to where the Pilot lay. The other pilot was blown clear and out of the corner of his eye he could see someone speeding to his side. Was it Hamish? Then someone was yelling "Get back! Get back! She's gonna blow!" He paid no heed. His task was obvious, to get the guy away and pretty bloody fast. The heat, smoke and fumes almost overcame him as he seized hold of the body. He gave no thought to any injury the Pilot might have sustained. The man weighed a ton. He heaved and strained and with strength that he knew was not his, but nevertheless flooded over him, managed to grab the Pilot's jacket and slide him up the beach. Away from the raging inferno. He dragged him until his strength gave out, then flung himself over the body sensing that time was running out. Then came the final explosion, with an almighty thunderbolt of a noise. His ears were ringing from the blast, his eyes smarting, and his face and ears were scorched. He could smell and taste smoke deep inside him and he could smell burnt flesh. He couldn't breathe. Then the pain hit him. He tried to remove the gauntlets, but he didn't have the strength. He sank down thinking so this is how it all ends, no more, no more, as he surrendered to the velvety, all-enveloping, suffocating darkness.

The storm had abated, and the winds were reduced to gentle zephyrs in comparison to what had gone before. Hamish was reading aloud at breakfast from the Aberdeen Gazette.

" ... in this night of high drama the island of Moraig, not for the first time, played a hero's part.

In a spectacular rescue, Blue Merlin, Drummer Alpha's standby vessel picked up 8 rig workers from the destabilised rig in the Dexter field.

The rig was on tow and had been caught out by the severe weather conditions. Her anchor chains had broken loose from the seabed, sea water had entered the ventilation system, and the rig was listing heavily.

Blue Merlin was driven on to the Moraig Rocks under the Moraig lighthouse, which was lashed by 100' waves, in unprecedented violent storm force conditions

The rescued rig workers and the ship's crew were in turn rescued from the stricken vessel by Moraig islanders, who put to sea despite the conditions and reached the safety of the lighthouse beach. The survivors were tended by islanders until the rescue helicopter arrived.

One of the rescue helicopters scrambled to the rig from RAF Rothesay, had made a perilous descent in total darkness, when the rig's emergency power failed. Having picked up 10 rig workers the helicopter was crippled with mechanical failure, which caused a fire on board.

This resulted in an unscheduled landing on Moraig. The rescued rig workers, none of whom were injured, jumped clear and ran up the beach to safety. The pilots were caught by the blast of the resulting explosion. The co pilot was blown clear but the handling pilot, Flt Lt Giles, took the force of the blast. He was dragged clear by the lighthouse cottage tenant, Mr James Cameron from London. All three men are now in the Special Burns Unit of the Royal Aberdeen Infirmary, having sustained severe burns and ...

The Police and The RAF Mountain Rescue Team are protecting the site, pending the arrival of the RAF's Accident and Recovery Flight, who will collect the parts for investigation, clean contaminated beach and water and return the site to its original condition...

The Board of Inquiry investigation is expected to take several months and ...

"So he's a hero after all!" said Hamish.

Katrina smiled. "Indeed he is!" thinking affectionately, and now do you understand why he had to come here you silly old fool?

And Hamish went off to engage in deedy conversation with the Laird, who had just returned and was disappointed to have missed out on so much drama. And such good publicity for Moraig and the islanders too!

Her patient stirred and the young woman drew near. He had been in intensive care for a few days and was now under her care in the Special Burns Unit. They were hopeful that his fingers could be saved. The driving gauntlets had taken the brunt of the burns and had been carefully cut from him in hours of surgery, but there was not the same assurance for his sight. The patient attempted speech, impossible through the cage and bandages on his face and neck. She collected herself.

"Mr Cameron! Good morning!" she said brightly. "We've been expecting you!" She thought, you've had quite a time of it but you're in my hands now. She pre-empted his next question.

"You're in the Royal Aberdeen Infirmary", she spared him, "the Special Burns Unit." There would be time enough for details. This was going to be a long job.

"You were extremely brave and dragged Flt Lt Giles, away from the blazing helicopter to safety. He's here too," omitting the list of his injuries. She thought, you saved him and I'm damn well going to save you, and you can bet on that.

"I'm Sister McClaren" she continued evenly, "but you had better call me Lennie. My name's Leonora."

★ ★ ★

The lighthouse, poised as ever on her rocks at the tip of her island, stared steadily out to sea, keeping her eternal vigil. Her bright beam rhythmically embracing her island in generous, protective swathes of light.

The official accident investigation had taken place and the island bore no sign of any dramas. Many scouring tides had ebbed and flowed since that dreadful night. But peace and tranquillity, the island's normality was now restored.

Katrina glanced up from the multicoloured strands of her intricate weaving to watch the flocks of geese lifting to circle the lighthouse, as if in farewell. They made their skein formations higher and higher until they disappeared from sight. She felt a twinge of sadness, as she always did, tempered by the surety that they would return as the year turned. She continued gazing out towards the tall, all seeing, indomitable edifice and reflected that under the lighthouse's everlasting protection, no doubt Moraig's destiny was unfolding just as it should and indeed to her watchful guardian's complete and utter satisfaction.

Evelyn Danbury

Ellen Fairchild

Ellen Fairchild was born and educated in the East End of London. After qualifying as a Nurse and Midwife she emigrated to Australia. Not being a sporty type and having a tendency to burn in the sun, she returned to the UK where she met and married her soldier husband. The following twelve years were spent as an Army wife and mother to their four children. On her husband's retirement from the Army the family settled in Norfolk.

Ellen, now a widow, is supported by a loving family and shares her house with a scruffy black cat and the occasional foster child.

Ellen Fairchild

A Good Day For It
- Ellen Fairchild -

'It's a good day for it,' Pam said as she pulled Joan's basket towards the till. The conveyer belt had broken down yet again.

'A good day for what?' Joan asked, looking up at the sun's rays streaming through the shop's dusty windows.

' The funeral of course. Haven't you read the news yet? Look here.' Pam removed a copy of the local news from the rack and flicked though the pages, stopping when she reached the obituaries.

'There,' she said pointing to several columns devoted to a Lieutenant Colonel Matthew Gunn. The headline ran: 'Local Hero Struck Down In His Prime.'

'Never heard of him. I don't even recognize him.' Joan peered at the grainy picture of a distinguished-looking, middle-aged man in military uniform. 'I've come out without my glasses. You'll have to tell me the details. Was he killed in action?'

'No, it says here, he died after a short illness. He's received lots of medals for gallantry. He was only fifty-five, died just before he was about to retire from the army, awful shame.'

'It happens too often.' Joan agreed. Hadn't her dear Fred died ten years ago, six months after they had moved to the village? It was their dream come true, to spend their twilight years together in the country.

' Has he got a family?'

'A wife and two sons,' said Pam, leaning across the counter towards her, her beehive hair creation nodding independently from her head, exposing the grey roots beneath the raven black.

I'm sure Pam would look a lot younger if she had a more modern hairstyle and didn't wear so much makeup, Joan thought, it looks as if she's applied it with a palate knife.

Pam lowered her voice as if confiding some great secret. The fact that the rest of the shop was empty obviously hadn't occurred to her. 'His mother still lives in the village, you know. Neat little woman, doesn't come in here very often. Keeps herself to herself. There's a daughter who visits her from time to time.' Straightening up, she began to scan Joan's groceries.

'This funeral will be special. I expect there'll be Top Brass attending.'

'What time does it start?'

'Twelve thirty,'

'I think I'll pay my respects and put some flowers on Fred's grave while I'm up there,' Joan said as she loaded her shopping trolley.

'If Sid agrees to look after the shop for an hour, I'll go up there too,' Pam said.

Joan paid for her goods.

'See you at the church, then, Pam.' And easing her trolley down the shop step, she disappeared into the sunny street.

★ ★ ★

It's a day more suited to a wedding or a christening. Joan thought, looking at the idyllic scene before her as she turned into Church Lane. The grey, stone church with its solid square tower was framed by an electric blue sky. The sheep, that earlier had been cropping the grass around the tombstones, were now grazing contentedly in the lush green fields beyond. The air was thick with the heady scents of summer. Busy insects hummed as they visited the wild flowers and the dog roses growing around the fallen and cracked monuments.

A selection of cars were parked on the verge by the church wall and further down the lane under the trees, a group of smartly uniformed soldiers stood by a minibus, chatting and smoking.

Some local people gathered around the lych gate, others leaned against the stone wall. A few, like Pam, had positioned themselves under a large oak tree in the church grounds, keeping a respectful distance from the porch where the mourners were gathering.

'We'll get a good view from here,' Pam said, as Joan arrived, a little out of breath.

The sound of heavy wheels on gravel heralded the arrival of the hearse followed by two black limousines. The soldiers stubbed out their cigarettes, straightened their uniforms and marched towards the hearse.

'That must be his widow and one of the sons,' Pam said, as a middle-aged woman in a black suit and black straw hat emerged from the first car, followed by a young man. An elderly woman supported by another young man stepped from the second car, followed by family and friends.

The soldiers gently eased the coffin from the hearse and onto their shoulders. The Union Flag was draped over it and single wreath of red roses and an officer's cap lay on top. Keeping in perfect step they carried it through the lych gate and up the path to the porch where the Vicar and the British Legion standard bearer waited to escort them into the church.

A photographer from the local news took pictures of the scene and then left.

As the service began some of the locals drifted away. Pam was about to leave when a small blue car drew up and stopped in the lane. Out stepped a dark haired woman. Clutching a large handbag she made her way to the church.

'That's probably the sister,' Pam said. 'Well, I've seen enough, I'm off now.'

'I have nothing to rush back for,' Joan said. 'I'm going to stay for a while and tend my Fred's grave.'

★ ★ ★

Carol felt the gaze of many curious eyes on her as she walked the path to the church. In the cool porch she stopped briefly. It had taken a lot of determination and soul searching to get this far. Was it too late to turn around and walk away? That would be the easy way out. She was here now and she would see it through to the end. With hands shaking, she pushed open the heavy door. The congregation, upstanding and in full flow, was singing the twenty third psalm: 'The Lord is My Shepherd.' No one turned to watch her as she entered and tiptoed to the last pew. The hymn finished and everyone sat down. A high ranking military man, his chest laden with medals, stepped up to the lectern. Clearing his throat he began.

'It is indeed a very sad occasion, for today, not only are we burying a personal friend of mine but also a man who was a courageous and exemplary soldier and a devoted husband,' (here he nodded towards Sylvia, seated in the front row,) 'and father to Daniel and Robert.' (- the two young men seated beside her.) The congregation listened in silence as the officer continued the eulogy, listing Matthew's distinguished career, all his achievements, medals and honours. The Vicar concluded the funeral service and as the final hymn was sung the coffin was once again hoisted by the bearer party and carried from the gloom of the church interior and out by a side door, into the brilliant sunshine.

The grave, newly dug and lined with green tarpaulin, had a commanding position on the prow of the hill with a panoramic view encompassing the church, the village and the surrounding meadows.

A soldier to the very end. Matthew would have approved of this plot, Carol thought as she picked her way around the tombs towards his final resting-place.

Sylvia and his sons stood close to the grave as the coffin was slowly lowered, the final prayers were said and a handful of soil was thrown on top. Sylvia stepped forward and threw a single red rose onto the coffin.

Do it, do it now, Carol told herself as she pulled a red rose from her bag. Battered but not broken, just like me, she thought, looking at the rose. Summoning up courage, she moved between the mourners and stepping to the edge of the grave, dropped it onto the coffin.

Having done what she had set out to do, Carol was turning to leave when Sylvia side stepped towards her.

'You were warned not to come, you were told you would not be welcome.' She hissed at Carol from under the brim of her hat.

' I have every right to be here,' Carol replied angrily, pushing past Sylvia, in her haste to avoid a confrontation. Sylvia wobbled, lost her balance and fell on top of the coffin.

Hearing the thud, Carol turned to see Sylvia lying spread-eagled on the coffin lid with her hat to one side. Having never met Sylvia before that day, Carol was struck by the ordinariness of her opponent. For a brief moment she even felt sorry for her. Then she remembered her own situation and the events leading up to Matt's death. She had not come with the intention of causing trouble; she merely wanted to say farewell to the man she loved. Dodging around the graves, she reached the path, leaving the officer on his knees helping Sylvia out of the hole and the mourners, close enough to witness what had happened, standing around in numbed silence.

Joan, unaware of the incident at the graveside, dozed on the memorial bench by the church porch when Carol rushed past her. Carol, forgetting to tread carefully over the cattle grid, caught the heel of her shoe between the metal bars. Tugging at it furiously, she could not free it.

'Let me give you a hand.' A youngish man with thinning fair hair bent down and carefully released the shoe. Handing it to her, Carol mumbled a quick 'Thank you,' and slipped it on. Not wishing to meet up with the people heading in her direction, she rushed off to her car.

As she was about to drive off, she took a last look at the church. She could see the tall figure of her rescuer sitting beside the old lady on the bench. There was something vaguely familiar about him. She was sure she had met him

before. Perhaps it was at the hospital where she worked.
Anyway, she told herself, it didn't really matter. The way
she felt now, nothing really mattered any more.

★ ★ ★

Dr. Gregory Turner parked his car outside the village
store and entered. Selecting a large box of chocolates, he
took them to the counter. The shop assistant put down her
knitting and stood up to serve him. He made his purchase,
and was just about to leave when the woman spoke.
'Aren't you Joan's son? Greg, isn't it?'
The doctor nodded and gave her brief puzzled smile.
He wondered how she knew him, he couldn't remember
meeting her or recall her weird hairstyle
'I'm Pam, a friend of your mum. I recognised you from
her photos. She's very proud of you, you know. Are you
visiting her?'
He nodded again.
'Well, you might still find her up at the church.'
He spoke. 'Doing the flowers for a wedding or some
special occasion I expect?'
'No' Pam said, 'she's up there watching the posh
funeral of an army officer.'
'Really!' he said, somewhat surprised, but then his
mother always had a soft spot for men in uniform, military
and royal pomp. Thanking her, he said he would look out
for his mother as he passed the church. He picked up the
chocolates and left.
As he drove slowly past the cars parked along the lane,
Greg spotted his mother seated on the bench outside the
church porch. The funeral must have reached its
conclusion. He could see people moving down between the

tombs towards the gate. Finding a space, he parked up and went to meet her.

'This is a lovely surprise. Why didn't you ring? You might have missed me.'

' I'm sorry I didn't let you know I was coming,' Greg said sitting down beside her.

'I have no excuse except pressure of work. I just happened to have a few hours free. It was a spur of the moment decision to come and see you.'

Joan studied her son. His once thick fair hair was showing signs of thinning and the worry lines had multiplied across his broad forehead.

'How are Annabelle and the children?'

'They are well. The children are looking forward to your stay with us next month. They all send their love.'

'So,' Joan asked, 'what brings you here at such short notice? Nothing serious I hope?'

'No, no, nothing serious.'

Joan wasn't convinced. She knew she would have to be patient and wait until he was ready to tell her what was on his mind.

'I'll drive you home Mum. We can talk, away from all this activity, in the peace of your garden.' Greg, his tall frame towering above his mother, took her arm in his and walked her to his car.

★ ★ ★

Reaching home by late afternoon, Carol, worn out by the events of the day, kicked off her shoes, flung herself on her bed and sobbed herself to sleep. When she woke it was dark and her bedroom was bathed in an eerie orange glow from the street lamps. Switching on her bedside lamp she was confronted by Matt's face smiling at her from its silver frame.

Holding the photo, she gazed at his face. He had always been a handsome devil, even more so in middle age. She had been desperate to be with Matt during his last hours but Sylvia had cruelly denied her that right. Why? she asked herself. It had been six months since she and Matt had last spent time together. They had planned for his retirement. He had been happy then, looking forward to civilian life. Or had he? Carol questioned. She had felt sure that their love for each other was strong enough to withstand the change. After all they had coped with far worse during their time together. With tears in her eyes, Carol remembered the happy times they had shared and that special day, the day they first met.

★ ★ ★

A face appeared at the gap in the curtain.

'Here fellas. There's a nurse stripping in here.'

The gap in the curtain widened and Carol became acutely aware of several eager young male faces watching her as she removed the bottom sheet from the bed. There followed a chorus of disappointed voices as the curtain was let fall back into place.

'Quit the teasing Matt, we really thought we were about to see the floor show, just then.'

'She was a bit of alright though,' another voice exclaimed

Blushing to the roots of her hair, Carol quickly stuffed the sheet into the dirty linen bag and hurriedly pushed the trolley into the sanctuary of the sluice. After a few minutes loitering in the sluice to regain her composure and to allow her burning face to cool down, Carol ventured out to the nurse's station.

'Nurse, you are to go for your break. On the way you are to take the patient in cubicle 7, a foot injury, suspected fracture, to x-ray. Ask them to get a porter to bring him back here with the report when they've finished. Here's his request form.' Sister thrust the blue card into Carol's hands and swished away, a vision in navy blue and starched white.

Carol looked at the name on the card.

'Matthew Gunn. Hmm,' she thought feeling the colour beginning to rise again in her cheeks. She selected a wheelchair and pushed it reluctantly to cubicle 7.

'Well if it isn't the stripping nurse. You're in luck Matt.' The casualty was sitting on the bed surrounded by several other young men in sweaty soiled sports gear.

'Leave her alone boys, we've had a laugh. Now that's enough.'

'Well you started it.'

'Ok, ok, I apologise for my unruly mates, Sister.' The occupant of the couch gave Carol a mischievous grin.

'I'm not a sister,' she said, noticing his attractive grey-green eyes.

'Staff Nurse?'

'No.'

'What are you then?'

'A third year student nurse,' Carol said, indicating the three chevrons on her sleeve.

'I'm to take you to x-ray, Mr Gunn. Please ease yourself into the wheel chair.'

'Well, don't you think that's kind of strange,' one of his companions commented, as Carol wheeled Matt from the cubicle. 'Sergeant nurse is looking after sergeant Gunn.'

Laughter echoed after them as the couple disappeared through the ward doors.

It was on their journey through the labyrinth of hospital lifts and corridors that Matt and Carol got to know each other better. During the following weeks and months they cemented their relationship. Nine months later, when Carol had completed her nurse training and Matt his promotion to staff sergeant, they were married.

It was after a few months of married life, it gradually dawned on Carol that she was not Matt's first love. His first love was the army and all things military. He was ambitious for promotion and determined to work his way up through the ranks to reach officer status.

★ ★ ★

Sylvia stared at the cloudless blue sky. She felt no pain; she was engulfed by an overwhelming sense of peace. Then reality dawned. She realised she was lying on top of Matt's coffin and two anxious faces were peering down at her.

'Are you alright Sylvia? Give me your hand.' The officer, kneeling on the edge of the grave, grabbed one hand and the vicar took the other. Together they pulled her from the hole.

'No bones broken?'

'No, thank God!' Sylvia replied shakily, brushing the soil from her suit and adjusting her hat.

Oh, the shame of it, the embarrassment of it all, she thought. That was no accident. It was deliberate.

'This is most unfortunate,' the officer said, pulling a flattened rose from the back of Sylvia's jacket and dropping it into the grave.

'Who was that woman?'

'I've never met her before. I think she must be one of Matt's old flames.' Well, it wasn't the exact truth, she certainly knew the woman's identity but she wasn't going to reveal it to the officer.

Hmm, the officer thought. Matt had a reputation with the ladies; it's a wonder more of them hadn't put in an appearance at his funeral.

'Take my arm, my dear,' he said. ' Let me escort you back to your car. You must be quite shook up.'

★ ★ ★

Carol stepped into the lift after her day shift at the hospital; the only other occupant was a tall fair-haired man. He smiled, then lowered his gaze to her identity badge

'Sister Carol Gunn?' He questioned: 'I believe we've met before?'

Carol studied his face.

'Yes, didn't you rescue me or rather my shoe from a cattle grid?'

'That's right. You seemed to have been in a bit of a hurry on that occasion.'

'You have a good memory,' she replied. 'It was last June.'

'With hindsight that day was a very significant one for me.' Looking again at her name badge, he asked: 'Were you related to the late Lieutenant Colonel?

He's very inquisitive, she thought, but then he is a doctor, Dr Gregory Turner to be precise. She had noted the title on his I.D. badge.

'Did you know him?' Carol asked.

'Well sort of, in an indirect way.'

The lift bumped to the ground floor.

'He was my husband,' Carol blurted out, as the doors opened.

'Your husband,' the doctor repeated, his grey –green eyes widening. Carol stepped forward into the flurry of the entrance hall and was about to disappear in the crowd when the Doctor called to her.

'Sister, are you in a hurry?'

'Well, I am rather keen to get home and put my feet up. It's been a long day.'

'If you could spare a few minutes, I would really like to have a quick chat. Over a cup of tea or coffee, perhaps?'

Carol was tired. She had buried herself in her work since the events of last June. She had cut herself off from Matt's family and her sons. Her work friends had entreated her to get some counselling because they were concerned for her health. They said she seemed to be constantly tired, short-tempered and prone to tears.

Perhaps, she thought, the young doctor could shed light on the events of that day which had caused her so much heartache, so in answer to the doctor's request, she agreed to stay for a little while. The young doctor and the reason for his being at the church on the day of Matt's funeral, intrigued her. She followed him into the W.R.V.S. cafe and, selecting a drink, sat down to hear what he had to say.

★ ★ ★

'You don't get it! You just don't understand do you?'

'Oh, I get it only too well.' Carol glared at Sylvia across the table.

'You stole my husband, turned my sons against me and deceived everyone into thinking you were the Lieutenant Colonel's wife.'

'I stole nothing,' Sylvia retorted, ' I merely filled the gap you left behind.'

'What gap? There was no gap in our relationship. Matt and I were making plans for his retirement.'

This is not going to work, Carol thought. I cannot talk to this woman. Doctor Turner had pressed her into meeting Sylvia. Her sons, with whom she was now reconciled, had also urged her to meet with Sylvia.

'This is a mistake, I should never have come,' she said, pushing her chair back.

'No don't go. Please stay. Let me explain,' Sylvia pleaded as Carol made to get up from the table. 'We need to sort this out. I need closure. You need closure.'

'There is no closure when you lose the one you love.'

Sylvia sighed. 'Yes, yes, you are right Carol. I loved him too.'

Carol looked at the woman seated opposite. We are about the same age, she thought. What on earth had he seen in her? Matt had asked her for a divorce some years ago but when she questioned if there was another woman, he had strongly denied it. He said he still loved her but the years apart had taken their toll. She had argued, with his retirement imminent, they would have all the time in the world to renew their relationship. It would be like a second honeymoon. She was sure she had convinced him and he had agreed. How had I missed the signs? she asked herself.

It was nearly three in the afternoon; the two middle-aged women were the only occupants in the bar room of the Old Ram Hotel.

'O.K.' Carol said sitting back in her chair. 'I'm listening.'

'As I'm not driving, I could do with something stronger than coffee. How about you?' Sylvia asked, pushing her cold coffee cup to one side.

'How about a glass of wine?' Sylvia had summoned a waitress before Carol had a chance to answer.

Sylvia took a sip of her wine, then began. 'I met Matt on his overseas posting about three years before he died. We went out a few times but it wasn't long before we moved in together. From the outset he said he was married. He told me he was lonely. He said you were busy in England looking after his sons and pursuing your own career. He said the two of you had grown apart.'

' We were only apart for the sake of our sons,' Carol asserted. 'Matt and I agreed that I set up home in England to ensure they had a loving and secure home life. We hadn't brought them into the world to send them away to boarding school. Matt came home whenever he could. We were happy. We bought our house together, we furnished it together and we planned retirement together. You made my sons lie and deceive me. For three years they knew of your existence and yet they kept it from me, from me, their mother.'

'No.' Sylvia said. 'We were very discreet. I would absent myself when they were visiting. They only discovered I existed a few weeks before Matt was rushed back to England for urgent medical tests. He told Daniel and Robert not to tell you about me. He said he would tell you himself, when the time was right. Didn't they tell you all of this?'

'Not all. I wanted to hear your version of events. Why was I not told he was so ill?'

'He didn't realise the severity of his condition. None of us did. He was told the surgery to repair the aneurysm was not without risk, so preparing for the worst outcome, should it occur, he planned his funeral with military precision. He gave me strict instructions that you were not to be informed, you were to have no part whatsoever. We were sure he would survive and none of that would be necessary.'

'How do I know you are telling the truth? You are blaming him and he's not here to defend himself. You just wanted the status of being the Lieutenant Colonel's widow with all the prestige and sympathy that goes with the title,' Carol said angrily.

'No! No! You've got it all wrong. We lived as man and wife. I attended all the military functions with him. His fellow officers and his men assumed I was his wife. Matt was happy to go along with that deception and so was I. He said he wanted to marry me and it was just a matter of time. They did not know of your existence and even if they did they probably thought you were his ex-wife.'

'But I wasn't his ex-wife.'

'You would have been had he lived,' Sylvia blurted out and immediately regretted it.

'I'm sorry that was very unkind of me.' She could see the effect of her thoughtless words had on Carol, who was now leaning on the table, her head in her hands.

' Here,' Sylvia said, topping up Carol's wine glass.' Have a drink. He did love you. His bravery was not in question. It was his reputation and standing amongst his men that stopped him from admitting you existed. Rank and status were everything to him. He did not want to lose their good opinion. If you had turned up he would have had to do a lot of explaining. It put me in a very awkward position when he died. I had to continue the lie. I don't blame you for pushing me into the grave, you must have wanted me dead.'

Carol raised her head and looked directly at Sylvia.

'Yes, I did wish you dead, but believe me it was an accident. I was in such a hurry to get away. You should have seen yourself, spread-eagled on Matt's coffin. What a sight. I wouldn't have wished that on my worst enemy and you were my worst enemy.' For the first time since their meeting Carol smiled.

'Sylvia, we have both lost the man we loved. I'm tired of it all. I think it's time we ended hostilities, laid him to rest and got on with our lives, don't you agree?'

'There is something I haven't told you,' Sylvia said. 'It's about Greg.'

Carol had wondered what connection the doctor had with Sylvia. He had told her he was a family friend and that he was concerned about her. He was keen for Carol to meet with her. It was he who had brought Sylvia to the venue.

'He's my son. I gave him up for adoption when I was sixteen.'

Carol gasped. His eyes, those grey- green eyes. She had been blind, it was obvious, Greg had his father's eyes. Greg was Matt's son.

'I was brought up in a garrison town.' Sylvia explained. 'Matt and his friends would buy sweets and cigarettes from my father's shop. I fell in love with him the first time I set eyes on him. I loved his mischievous grin and his lovely grey-green eyes. We dated for a few months then suddenly, without warning, his regiment was posted abroad. We lost touch. Then I discovered I was pregnant. My parents were distraught; they insisted that I should have the child and give it up for adoption. When, quite by chance, I met Matt again, I told him he had another son somewhere. Then last year, Greg found me, sadly too late to meet his father.'

How strange, Carol thought. Sylvia had parted with her son but had ended up being reunited with his father, while she, Carol, had refused to be parted from her sons and had lost their father.

★ ★ ★

Who'd have thought it would have turned out like this, Joan said to herself as she adjusted her wide - brimmed, rose - covered peach hat. She had spent most of the morning decorating the church with summer flowers. Now suitably decorated herself, she took a last look in the mirror and stepped out into the sunshine.

'Come on grandma, or we'll be late,' young voices called to her.

Never in a million years had she imagined she would experience a day like today. It had all started on the day of the Lieutenant Colonel's funeral. That day Greg had told her he had decided to search for his birth mother. Ever since she and Fred had adopted him as a baby they feared they would lose him one day.

Looking at Greg, Annabelle and the children waiting for her by the car, she knew her fears were groundless.

' It's a good day for it,' she said, beaming, as she got into the car. They were going to a Christening, no ordinary Christening, a posh christening, as Pam would say. This time Joan was not going as an onlooker but as a guest. Old Mrs Gunn would be there, Sylvia and Carol would be there. Carol's sons, Daniel with his girlfriend Kate and Robert with his wife Lisa and the star of the show, their beautiful baby daughter with grey-green eyes, Matilda Gunn.

The Peashooter
- Ellen Fairchild -

S electing the largest cow parsley, the boy snapped it at the base, whorled it around like a baton for a few minutes, then stripped it of its flower head and scattered the seeds on the path. Squinting through the hollow stem, he decided it was too long, so he removed several unwanted segments and threw them into the hedge. The remaining dry hollow tube was about 10 inches in length. Holding it up to his right eye, he scanned the horizon, imagining he was a pirate captain searching for a treasure ship. No treasure ships to be seen, only cows munching quietly in the field. Targets, he decided, and pointing it at the nearest cow he blew through the tube. Now he was a South American Indian shooting poison darts at his enemy. What was missing? The ammunition, of course. Walking slowly along the path he studied the hedge. He rejected the rose hips and hazels; they were unripe and too big. Other flower seeds were too soft or too lightweight. He was trying to remember the seeds his Dad had used a few summers before when he had crept up behind the family, stinging the backs of their necks with small hard brown seeds. It was then that he spotted the hawthorn bush. The branches held clusters of the small brown seeds where once the creamy flowers had hung. Scrambling up the bank, he went to grab a handful. Ouch! A thorn caught his finger. Examining his finger closely, he sucked it, examined it again then dismissed it. With more care he stuffed his pockets with the little seeds. Now for some target practice he decided, as he jumped down onto the path. Putting a few of the seeds in his mouth he then proceeded to blow them at the metal farm gate. They made satisfying pinging sounds. Good, he congratulated himself, I'll show those country boys I'm as good as them.

He climbed through a gap in the hedge and sauntered down a well-trodden path, fringed with tall waving grasses. Through the trees he glimpsed the house, his house, his new home in the country.

'Great!' he yelled, leaping into the air, 'Dad's home.' He could see the green and red land rover parked by the front door. Putting on speed he raced down the gravel drive, through the side gate, skidded to the back of the house and shot in the back door.

'Are you stopping, Dad?' he asked breathlessly as he flung himself at his dad who was standing in the kitchen.

Giving him a big hug and ruffling his hair his dad replied:

'Not this time son, I'm on my way to a job up North. I've just popped home for a cup of coffee. Can't stay long.'

'Go and wash your hands.' His mother placed a plate of steaming food on the table. 'You've been dawdling again. You haven't got much time to eat your dinner and get back to afternoon school, so you will have to hurry.'

The family had moved to the village in Norfolk two months ago. The boy loved the peaceful country life. He liked going to the village school and being able to go home for dinner each day along the lane and through the field. He didn't miss the hustle and bustle of the Military Camp and the crowded married quarters. Everything was perfect except his Dad would be working away from home for another year until he retired from the Army.

'If you eat your dinner quickly I'll drop you back to school on my way out of the village,' his dad said as the boy tucked into his meal.

'Great!' Now his new school friends would get to meet his dad. When he had first told them his dad was a soldier, they'd teased him.

'How many has he killed? That's what soldiers do, don't they? They learn to fight and kill.'

'Boom, rat-tat-tat-tat-tat, you're dead.' They'd laughed and run off, pretending to shoot anything and everything in their way. He'd been crestfallen. He loved his Dad. He was proud of his Dad. Now at last he had the chance to show those country boys what a kind and gentle man his Dad was.

'Come on son.' his Dad called out. 'Time to go.'

Forgetting about his peashooter, the boy hurriedly kissed his Mum and rushed out to the land rover. He failed to notice the dark cycles round her eyes, her worried expression or the fact that she had barely spoken to his dad all the while he was eating his dinner.

'Up you go,' his dad said, helping him into the passenger seat. The boy looked to see if his Mum had come out of the house to see them off, but she was nowhere to be seen. Raindrops splashed on the windscreen as they moved off. By the time they reached the school gates, the rain was falling heavily. To his utter dismay, the playground was empty, the afternoon classes had begun and he was late.

Hiding his disappointment, he hugged his Dad. Standing in the rain he waved goodbye and watched as the land rover took off down the lane. He stood watching until all that could be seen of the land rover was the lettering on its rear. In bright red letters on a white background it spelt out Bomb Disposal.

Francesca Hamilton

Francesca Hamilton is a lawyer by profession, having trained and practised as a Barrister in London before returning to her native Norfolk after she married. Upon her return she re-qualified to practice as a Solicitor. Currently, Francesca lives with her husband and two young sons, and writes whenever she has a spare moment!

Francesca Hamilton

The Meeting House
- Francesca Hamilton -

T he Meeting House stands alone on its own little triangular pavement between two quiet thoroughfares: one leads to London, and the other, to the country. It is made of red brick and has five sash windows; four of which possess their own corner of the house, the fifth, alone, in the middle of the house above the large double doors. A tall black lamppost stands at its front, just to the right of the doors. But other than that, the house is no different to those which stand to its left and right. All that is, except for its name, and the fact that my father was found murdered there.

★ ★ ★

My mother and I are sitting in the morning room – she is sewing and I am looking out of the window. I am hoping to see my father. I chanced upon him having an argument with a stranger last night. He left the house suddenly. Now, I fear for his safety.

It was a hot, balmy summer's night. I could not sleep; my room was stifling even though the windows were wide open. My mouth was as dry as cloth; I needed a drink.

I was walking down the stairs to go to the kitchen when I heard voices coming from my father's library. I didn't take much notice of them at first – my head was too thick with sleep to pay attention to anything other than getting myself down the stairs safely.

But as I reached the last few steps, I could hear the voices more clearly: two voices, both male, and one belonged to my father. They were arguing. I say they were arguing – my father's voice was raised but the other man's voice was calm; he held his temper in a controlled, sinister way. He was trying to blackmail my father – he kept saying that my father would not want me - me! - to learn of his secret and so my father had better pay him. My father would have none of it. And so the man left, followed shortly after, by my father. They went to the Meeting House: a place where my father goes often. I did not hear what the secret was, but it was something terrible, of that I am sure – otherwise, my father would not have followed this man.

'George!' My mother's voice wakes me from my thoughts. I look up to see her walking towards my uncle, Sir George Felton. But then she stops – suddenly, as though she has walked into glass. She lets out a small cry. My uncle's face is ashen, his eyes are heavy and black. He is twisting the hat he holds in his hand. He opens his mouth to speak but says nothing. I walk over to where they are standing.

'I'm sorry,' he breathes. My mother holds her hand to her mouth and collapses onto the chair by her side. She stares down at the rug, her eyes darting backwards and forwards. I don't understand why, as he has said nothing to make her react in this way.

'Uncle?'

My uncle looks up at me in astonishment, as though he had not seen me before.

'Your father is dead.'

That is what he says; four words. Your father is dead. And I stop too – just like my mother. I look at him – perhaps I misheard. But his face confirms it. My father - my wonderful father - is dead!

My mother is weeping now; her shoulders are shaking, her head still cast down.

I feel sick. I hold onto the chair where my mother is sitting, and I feel myself swaying backwards and forwards. My uncle reaches out to steady me. He sits me down in the chair next to my mother's. I stare at the rug, my eyes tracing the pattern of the roses whilst my mind races - back to the argument I overheard the night before. I feel my body moving forward, my head is spinning. I can hear my uncle's voice but I cannot understand what he is saying; his words are one big, long noise.

He puts a glass to my mouth. It has a sharp smell and makes me recoil, but my uncle fixes the glass to my lips and forces the liquid down. It hits the back of my throat like a ball of fire and I cough. He strokes my back. I need some air. I stand; my uncle's arms are under mine, steadying me. I walk to the window and breathe in the air, holding on to the sill. I take long deep breaths and breathe them out slowly.

Then it is all gone and I feel calm. I stand tall, and turning to face my uncle ask, 'How?'

My uncle is shocked. He looks at me, his nineteen year old niece, and cannot believe that I should ask such a question.

'How did my father die?' I ask in a steady voice, my back straight, my eyes staring straight into his. He stammers, but I wait for his response.

'He was murdered,' he says at length. 'At the Meeting House. His body was found there this morning. They called me straight away.'

I gasp. My breath winds me and I stumble against the windowsill, but I don't take my eyes off my uncle.

'I know who did this.' I whisper, my voice hoarse.

My uncle stares at me.

'I know who did this,' I repeat, not sure whether he heard me the first time. 'Last night...,' I continue, 'last night, I heard Papa argue with another man. He had a secret: something about Papa. Something he thought Papa would want to keep a secret. He was trying to blackmail Papa; he asked him for £10,000. Papa refused to pay him. They fought. The man told Papa to meet him at the Meeting House. I heard him go. I heard them both go...' I sit on the window seat and look out of the window.

'Did you get a look at the man?' my uncle asks.

'No.' I shake my head. 'It was too dark. I hid behind the dining room door; I did not want him to see me. I saw only his coat – a long coat, dark – like buckskin; like a night watchman's coat. And a hat – a large brimmed hat, and boots like a stable hand's. But I heard his voice – and I would recognise it again... there was a wicked calmness about it...'

My uncle puts his hands on my shoulders. 'Do not trouble yourself further, child. Justice Gage has appointed me constable. I will find out who the murderer is and bring him to justice.' Then he turns to my mother and says, 'Now I must take your leave.' He kisses my mother's hand and without looking over at me, walks towards the door.

'Uncle?' He turns. 'How did he die?'

My mother shrieks. 'Clara! How can you be so morbid? Is it not enough that he is dead?'

'How did he die?' I repeat. There is a silence in the room as my uncle tries to work out how to tell me.

'His throat was cut.' My mother lets out another shrill cry and my uncle goes to her. 'He wouldn't have felt a thing,' he lies as he kneels down at her side and strokes her hand. 'It would have been over in no time.'

I know this is not true; I have read too many of my father's books to know that this is not true. He would have put his hands to his throat and realised, as he gasped for air and his lungs filled with blood, that he would not recover: he was going to die.

'I shall get to the bottom of this,' my uncle declares as he rises to his feet again and makes for the door. 'I shall find your father's murderer, you need not trouble yourself.'

How little did the Justice know – how little did I know – the conflict of interest which would arise by my uncle's appointment as constable, in charge of my father's murder investigation.

★ ★ ★

Today is the 2nd July 1831. It has been precisely three weeks since my father was murdered, and I have relived every moment of the night he died as if it took place only yesterday. I have seen myself walking into the room to confront the man who was to murder my father and ask him to share with me the secret he feels my father is so damned by that he should rather pay a small fortune than

- 95 -

risk his life. Or else, I have walked into the room once the man has gone, and persuaded my father not to go out to meet him; that whatever his secret, it is one that will not make me think any the less of him. And I have seen the face of my father's murderer; the face hidden under the wide brim of his hat, overshadowed by the darkness of the hour.

But it is mostly in my dreams that I see my father fighting for his life as the knife comes down upon his throat and slashes it with such force that my father is thrown to the ground and holding onto his throat, stares in disbelief at his attacker, whilst he chokes on his own blood. And I see the face of his attacker laughing at him, his hard, brown, weathered skin crumpled with laughter, his teeth rotten in his gums. And when I have woken myself with my crying out, I sit and wonder what it was that my father could possibly have been guilty of; such a secret that he risked his life to keep it from me?

I am sitting in the morning room with my mother; she is sewing and I am trying to read. I cannot concentrate, and so I find myself staring out of the window, wondering why it is that my uncle has not been able to find the man who murdered my father? I know that my uncle and my mother have met in these last three weeks, and from the closed doors and hushed tones, believe them to have spoken of the murder, though no-one will tell me what has been discussed.

'Mama? Have you heard from uncle?'

My mother sighs and putting down her sewing straightens her back and looks over towards the window at me.

'Get away from the window, child! Have you nothing better to do than idle around staring out of the window like a common whore?'

'Mama!' I recoil at her words.

'Where is your embroidery? If you hadn't spent so long looking into your father's books, you may have some intelligent conversation to share with your poor widowed mother! Here! Go and buy some silks and cloth from Madame Pantoufle, and I shall show you again how to embroider neatly.' She reaches into her purse which is lying at the side of her, and offers two coins to me.

'I could play for you...?' I venture; I am not enthralled at the idea of visiting anyone let alone Madame Pantoufle.

'Goodness child, no. This is not a time for playing tunes. My nerves are still most fragile; I have not the patience to hear your mistakes.'

She gestures for me to take the coins from her.

'What of my uncle, though. It has been three weeks...'

'I am well aware how long it has been since your dear Papa's passing. Have I not been a widow since that time? Have I not had to sit here keeping myself out of all polite society? Have I not had to bear the visits by those who come merely to see how I look and dress? Do I not know how long it is that I have had to wear these awful clothes? Believe me, every time I look down at my skirts or hear this dreadful material swish as I walk, I am reminded of my pitiful state.'

I put out my hands to take the coins from her; it is clear to me that she will not tell me what she and my uncle have been discussing. But rather than give the coins to me, she pulls her hand away quickly and says:

'Mind you get the brighter colours. I don't want any more drabness in this house – I have enough with my own melancholy.'

'Yes mama.' I promise and turn to walk to the door.

'And be sure to ask Madame Pantoufle what news she has for me; I am quite lonely here on my own with only my grief to keep me company.'

Gossip. Idle gossip; that is the reason why I am to go to Madame Pantoufle's shop. It is just as well for there is no more likelihood of me learning to sew properly than my mother finding the patience to teach me. But I am glad to be out of her company, and away from her temper. She has no more grieved for my father than she would for a common thief. His death has been nothing more than an inconvenience for her, shutting her away from society and attention. Had it not been for the period of mourning that she has to endure, I would rather have said that she views his death as a relief.

★ ★ ★

I have to walk past the Meeting House on my way into town. I am not looking forward to seeing the place where my father was murdered; to see people going in and out, getting on with their business and their lives whilst mine has been so irrevocably halted. My heart hangs heavily.

As I draw closer to the House, my pace slows. I take a deep breath as I round the corner and the House comes into sight. To my surprise, it looks as innocuous as it did in the days before my father's death. There are no shadows cast over it to hide its shame. It is no more worn down by its past, than the large stone steps which lead to its doors. It sits in the sunlight, its red bricks as warm as coals in a grate, its windows bright, reflecting the sun as it shines.

I stand and stare at it as though it would reveal its secret to me. I care nothing for the people who stare at me as they pass by. Some of them stop and look with me, but quickly move on when they see no spectacle. But I cannot move on.

It is not somewhere I can simply pass on my way into town any more: it owes me an explanation – it became a part of me the day my father died within its walls.

I am standing at the front of the triangular pavement facing the House. I can see into the windows; the maids are scuttling around the tables laying them for dinner, the men are wiping the glasses. The curtains hang elegantly at the windows, long and serene; it is a picture of innocence and decorum.

I imagine my father in the house, sitting in a large leather chair, smoking a cigar and sharing a joke with friends; perhaps drinking whisky and nibbling at some refreshment. Or else, playing bridge, concentrating hard on the cards in front of him or the faces of his companions, watching their reactions as he lays down his cards. I know that face he pulls when he is defeated, when his velvety brown eyes turn hard like the bark on a tree, and his smile becomes fixed and artificial.

And then the House becomes blurred, and I realise that tears are flowing down my cheeks, and all I want to do is crumple into a ball, right here on the pavement.

'Clara? What are you doing here, my dear?' It is my uncle's voice; what a welcome sight his face is! 'My dearest girl,' he calls me as he sees the tears running down my face, and he puts his arm around me and walks me away from the House. 'Let's get you some tea.'

We walk to the tearooms, just a short distance from the House, and having sat me down, he says, 'That is why we have a period of mourning. For you to stay away from society and gather yourself together. What are you doing coming out so soon?' His voice is tender and kind.

'Mama could not bear my company any longer. I am come out to buy silks.'

My uncle nods sympathetically.

'Right!' He gathers himself together. 'Tea I think? And a cake or two as well. You need to keep your spirits up, and I could do with something to keep my stomach from growling'. I smile at him, and although I have stopped crying I can feel where my tears have fallen by the tightness of my skin.

My uncle orders our refreshments as I gather myself together.

'Uncle?' I enquire as the serving girl walks away.

'Yes, my dear?'

'Why were you at the Meeting House? Have you not concluded your business there?'

My uncle looks away from me.

'Have you news of my father's murderer?'

He remains silent, hesitant.

'I would rather hear from you, what it is you have discovered. My mother is reluctant to talk about my father at all.'

My uncle nods but still says nothing.

'Please uncle. I must know what has happened. I must believe that you have caught him; that he is to be tried and brought to justice. My mother will not mind – indeed she will be glad not to have to tell me herself.'

'I...I...' He sighs and shakes his head. 'There is no news.'

I laugh in disbelief, but his face remains fixed.

'I have questioned many who were at the House that night and no one will admit to seeing anything unusual. Many say they saw you father at the House and they saw him leave fit and well.' He shrugs his shoulders.

I flinch and catch my breath, sinking into my chair. 'But how can that be, Uncle?' I whisper, tears rising to my eyes. He looks at me in surprise; he had not imagined that I would challenge his words. 'He left our house very late, I know, but not so late that the House would have emptied of its occupants.' I can feel the blood rising in my face, I can hear the anger in my voice.

Before my uncle has to say anything, the tea arrives. I can see the relief on his face.

'Surely the servants saw him re-enter?' I continue, not caring who may hear. 'Did none of them question his return at such a late hour?'

My uncle's eyes remain fixed on the tea. I lean forward gathering strength from his silence. 'Uncle? Did no-one notice a stranger enter the House that night?'

My uncle finishes pouring the tea, then places his hands in his lap and slowly lifts his eyes off the tea tray and looks at me. He opens his mouth, but again says nothing.

I feel the blood rushing back to my face: I want to shake the words out of him! But he looks down again and shifts in his chair. 'I cannot say…'

'Cannot or will not?' I hiss leaning forward in my chair. The lady and gentleman at the table next to us stop their conversation and look over at me. Now, it is my turn to bow my head and look down in embarrassment. I sit back in my chair and fiddle with my fingers as I try to compose myself.

'Here, have some tea.' My uncle pushes a cup towards me and I pick it up and bring it to my lips. I am so angry I can hardly stop the tea from spilling into my lap. I devour the tea whilst keeping my eyes fixed on the edge of the table. My heart is pounding, my cheeks tingling with heat.

We sit in silence until the couple next to us start up their conversation again.

'There is nothing I can tell you.' My uncle repeats.

'Why is it you have never asked me more about the argument I heard my father have with the stranger in my own home, the night he died? The details of the conversation? The sound of the man's voice; his accent, his words?' My uncle just sits shaking his head and says nothing. I put down my teacup: it is useless to try any more.

'Thank you for the tea,' I say, my voice composed. 'I have an errand to run.' I rise from my chair before he can object to my leaving, and steadying myself with the table, I walk out slowly and deliberately, head held high though my stomach churns.

★ ★ ★

I do not know where to go now. I am so angry with my uncle: I am sure he knows more than he is prepared to tell me, but what it is, I cannot say.

I turn away from the Tea House and wander the dusty streets of the town trying to figure out why my uncle will not tell me what is going on; what it is that my uncle is hiding from me? And then I stop suddenly in the street. Of course! He must know of my father's secret!

But that doesn't explain why my uncle cannot find out anything about my father's murderer. I cannot believe that there wasn't anyone at the Meeting House who didn't see or hear something unusual.

I walk on, paying no attention to where I am going. I wander further and further away from the town, down back streets, far from the crowds. Without knowing it, my feet have brought me to the churchyard where my father is buried. It is a quiet little churchyard; the church, St Andrew's, sits in the middle of two lawns. It is an attractive building, made of the local Norfolk flint. I walk around the nave to the furthest side of the church towards my father's grave. It is hidden in the corner of the churchyard under the dappled shadow of a willow tree. He is buried in the family vault; a magnificent white stone monument. Around the grave is a small pathway made of gravel, and at the front of the vault is a vase where flowers can be left. I shall go to his grave; there at least, I will find some peace.

I am so embroiled in my thoughts, that I don't see her at first. And she has not noticed the stirring of the grass under my feet, for she turns suddenly and looks up at me with fear in her eyes. I stop as confused as she is scared, and open my mouth to ask what she is doing at my father's grave? But there is something in her eyes which catches my breath and stops me speaking; she has a familiar look to her, but I am sure I have not seen her before. She is dressed poorly, with a large brown bonnet on her head and shawl over her shoulders.

We look at each other for only a few seconds before she turns and runs towards the lych gate at the bottom of the graveyard, and out into the alleyway.

I look down at my father's grave; pink foxgloves have been interwoven with the yellow roses that I left only a week ago.

'Stop!' I call, but she is gone. I run after her; she is going towards the Vicarage. I can see her ahead of me; she is no longer running but her movements are swift. But at the Vicarage, she turns towards the town. I speed up, not wanting to lose sight of her; I am afraid that when she reaches the street she will disappear in the crowd.

I find my way to the street and looking down towards the town see that she has crossed over the road and is weaving her way through the people as deftly as a needle sews through cotton.

Finally, I see her enter Marsham Street and walk away from the shops and in the direction of my home. Keeping my eyes fixed on her, I too weave my way through the crowds. She is walking more slowly now, and I am gaining upon her. I slow down too, not wanting to be seen by her in case she takes flight again. Then she stops. She waits for a horse and carriage to pass by then she crosses the road. And then I stop, suddenly. She has entered the Meeting House.

★ ★ ★

I wander home and hope to go straight up to my room and lie down. When I arrive, however, I see my uncle's chaise parked on the gravel driveway in front of the house. My heart sinks: he is bound to have told Mama of the scene I caused at the tea rooms, and she will reprimand me and not speak to me for the rest of the week.

I enter the front door and start to walk up the stairs when the door to the drawing room opens.

'Clara?' It is my uncle calling me. 'Clara, ah there you are! Come down, my dear, do. You had quite worried me going off like that. You have been gone some time!'

I obey my uncle and walk down the stairs again, and into the drawing room. My mother is reclined on the chaise longue holding her handkerchief up to her nose, trying to look as if she is upset, though in truth I can see no evidence of her having shed a single tear.

'Do sit down, my dear.' My uncle gestures to one of the chairs near to my mother. 'Where have you been?' He enquires politely.

'To my father's grave.'

He clears his throat.

'I have explained to your mother that we have been unable to obtain any information as to your father's murder despite extensive enquiries, and it will be my recommendation that the case is closed. I feel it is the best for you and your dear mother.' He finishes quickly.

My mother lets out a large sob and starts to dab the corners of her eyes with her handkerchief. My uncle looks at me tentatively; I know he is expecting me to shout or scream at him, but I am too numb by the day's events to make any response.

'I have to think of your mother's nerves,' he continues.

'May I go now?'

They look at me in surprise.

'Why, yes, of course!' My uncle answers. I see the relief on his face. I get up and walk out of the room, closing the door behind me.

★ ★ ★

I slip out of the house as soon as I hear my mother retire to her room for the night. I am going to the Meeting House. I am going to find the woman I saw at the churchyard and confront her.

I have borrowed my maid's cloak. It is thick and heavy, too heavy for this heat, but I cannot wear mine if I am not to be detected. I pull the hood over my head as I close the door and walk out onto the street. It is quite deserted. I can smell the evening air as I walk along the street; a cool, fresh, earthy smell. A heavy dew has fallen already.

By the time I reach the Meeting House, I have built up quite a sweat. The House still has its windows open though very little sound comes from inside: most of the visitors appear to have gone home. I linger in the shadows of a tall brick wall on the pavement opposite the House.

I am not there for more than five minutes when I hear the chimes of the church bells; it is eleven o'clock. The windows to the House are being closed. I cannot see well enough who is closing them. Then I see the lights being snuffed out and the House turns to darkness. I shall wait a couple of minutes more, and if there is no movement, I shall cross to the back of the House and go down the alleyway and in through the servants' door.

I watch the House intently, barely blinking for fear that someone who knows me will come out of the Meeting House and find me. My heart thumps as I wait. Finally, it is time to go.

I cross over the road, my heart beat rising. The fabric of my dress sticks to me. I step into the alleyway at the back of the House, and stand hard up against the wall listening for any noise or sign that someone may be around, but my heart is beating so fast I find it difficult to hear anything else. I creep further forward. There is something soft and sticky under my feet. I lift my skirts and tiptoe forward. The alley smells strongly of urine; it chokes me. I hold my cloak over my nose with one hand, my skirts still held in the other. My eyes start to smart with the stench. I want to vomit.

Eventually, when I am about a quarter of the way into the alley I see a small ray of light coming from a doorway. Someone may still be awake: if they are, I shall ask where this woman sleeps. They will suspect nothing; I am dressed like a servant myself. I tiptoe further towards the light and when I am almost at the door I stop again and listen. Still, there is silence. I slide towards the doorway, and then I slip into the House.

The House is stuffy and smells of cigars and alcohol. It is almost completely dark, except for one candle which is still alight in a holder on the wall in front of me, and another on a table in a room to my right. Along the wall which leads to this room, cloaks and hats are hanging on pegs. They are all made of a coarse material, similar to my maid's; they must belong to the servants who live here. I move over to the cloaks and hide myself between them: if anyone comes along the corridor, I will not be seen easily in the shadows.

From the safety of my hiding place, I look around. I can see quite clearly into the room to my right. It is a scullery; a large room with a stone floor, similar to the one I am standing on at the moment. In front of me, the hallway leads into the main entrance of the Meeting House; it is a large carpeted area with two, perhaps three doors leading off it, and stairs which extend above my head.

To my left, behind the door I have just entered, are two more doors, side by side. One of these must lead up to the servants' rooms.

Taking a deep breath, I tiptoe towards the doors. I shall try the door on the left first. I put my ear to it and listen for any movement; there is none. I place my fingers onto the latch and I guide it up and out of its resting place. I then pull on the handle and open the door. I peer into the blackened space. There are stairs, but they lead downwards into the cellar.

My heart sinks and I step back and closing the door as quietly as I can, move to the door on the right. Again, I place my ear hard up against the wood and listen for any noise. Not a sound. Again, I press my fingers onto the latch and guide it upwards. There is a clank this time as the latch hits the metal case above it. I hold my breath and listen. To my relief I have not disturbed anyone.

I pull the door towards me. It creaks as it opens. I wait. Nothing. I pull it again. It creaks again and I wait. Still, I hear nothing. I slip inside leaving it open behind me.

The stairs are immediately in front of me. They are narrow and winding. I make my way up the stairs slowly and carefully, all the time keeping my hands flat against the cool brick walls on either side. I can see no light above me – I shall be able move around without being detected.

Finally, when the stairs have almost turned full circle, I reach the top. The wall to my right falls away and leads onto the wooden floor. I steady myself against the wall to my left and wait to catch my breath, whilst looking around me.

In front of me there is a long leaded window; it is not one I had noticed when looking at the House from the outside. It is open slightly and I can feel the coolness of the night through it: it is a welcome relief! To my right there is a corridor with a door at the end. I can see a small, flickering light coming from under the door. I can hear shuffling and hushed voices. To my left is a darker corridor, longer than the one to my right. I can just make out a door at the end and two other doors at either side.

I step up onto the landing and turn towards the voices, steadying myself against a low lying chest that sits under the window. I inch forward, careful not to make any noise with my footsteps, when suddenly the door at the end of the corridor opens. Without thinking I crouch down and shuffle backwards to the end of the chest and hide behind it, my head in my hands.

'Get out! I don't want you round me no more, do you hear?' It's a woman's voice; she is speaking in a forced whisper.

'Come inside and close the door before you wake the others.' It was the stranger who argued with my father on the night of his death! I bite into my cloak to stop myself screaming.

'I will not! I will not do it, do you hear?'

The door slams shut and I am saved. I breathe out again and look up, my heart still thumping. Do I stay or go? I am scared, but also in a fury that the man who murdered my father is here; he has the audacity to stay in town after what he has done! I shall confront him! But if I do, he may kill me too! I shall go to my uncle – he will be able to gather some men together and come back to arrest him.

I stand up and watching the door, creep to the top of the stairs. I can still hear the muffled voices arguing in the room. I hold my foot out to go down the stairs then hesitate. What if my uncle comes back too late and the man has gone? I cannot let him leave. I take a deep breath and walk steadily towards the room, my fists clenched in determination.

I can hear them still arguing as I reach the door.

'It's not to be done, John! Leave them alone. They've already lost their husband and father, why do you want to give them more misery?'

'It's our due, 'Liza. It's what's due to you! The money's nothin' to them. They've got more than you and I could ever dream of. They wouldn't even miss it!'

'And will you stop there? When we get the ten thousand off them? No, I didn't think so. It's not about the money any more is it? You killed him. You murdered him! We have to leave now while we still have the chance. You're lucky you haven't been arrested already! We've waited long enough. There's no need for us to stay now – if we leave now, no-one will think it has anything to do with the murder.'

The words hit me like a stone. I stagger backwards, a wave of sickness rushing from my stomach.

'John! John! Where are you going?'

They are moving towards the door!

'If we can't get the money off them, then we shall take the girl!' He laughs, deep and hollow.

'What? But why?'

Now I am in danger! I must leave – and quickly! I pick up my skirts and lunge forward, but before I am able to steal away down the stairs I hear the door latch go: it is too late! I crouch down again and hide behind the chest under the window.

'Get some sleep. We'll speak of this again tomorrow. Get off me woman! I'm hardly likely to steal her from her bed!'

I hear a crash and the woman crying out in pain. I hold my breath and turn my face into my cloak, hoping that I will not be seen. I hear footsteps coming in my direction – a heavy shuffle getting louder. I cannot see where he is but I sense that he is quite close. I want to cry out; to scream and push past him, to get out and be safe. But I know that. I can't – I haven't got the strength to carry myself down the stairs. I bite my lip trying to stop myself panting. The echo of his footsteps rings through my head. Then he stops. I can hear his breathing getting closer and closer. He is bending down towards me. He has seen me!

'What have we here then?' I can smell his alcoholic fumes. I imagine him swaying over me as he tries to work out who it is under the cloak. Then he lets out a low guttural laugh. He kicks at me, and despite myself I let out a small cry.

'Looks like one of your friends 'ere 'as 'ad a bit too much to drink!'

There is a lighter patter of footsteps as the woman follows him.

'Aye,' she says. 'Happen it's Moll. Now get yerself gone. I'll deal wi' her.' Her voice is shaky and uncertain. I hear him huff and then he turns and walks down the stairs, his boots heavy and slow. At the bottom of the stairs he shuffles.

'An' don't you go sayin' a word to no-one 'Liza, you hear?' He calls up.

'Aye! Be gone!'

More shuffling, and then the door closes and he is gone.

I look up from where I sit. The woman is still looking down the stairs. Then she turns and looks over at me. The moonlight falls on her face and I recognise her; it is the woman I saw at the graveyard.

'Moll? Is that you?' She puts her hand on my arm and gently shakes me. I look up at her and she jumps back, not expecting me to have moved so quickly.

'Who are you?' she asks. I can hear the fear in her voice. I don't know whether I should reply or run past her. We stand facing each other for a moment then I gesture to her room and she leads the way.

I close the door behind us. Her room is small. She walks to the furthest end of the room and stands behind her bed. On a small table to her left stands a single candle. She sees me looking at it and grabs it, holding it in her hand like a weapon. It is then that she sees my face. She gasps, almost dropping the candle.

'What do you want? You shouldn't be here!' Her voice sounds more urgent than frightened.

'I want to know why he murdered my father.' I answer. My voice is calm. She looks at me, shocked by what I have said.

'I cannot tell you. You must leave. It is not safe for you here. If he comes back he will kill us both.'

'I am not afraid,' I lie. 'I must know why!'

She looks at me, and tries to work out whether I mean what I say or not. She bites her lip and sighs. 'Not 'ere, not now. It's too dangerous.'

'When?'

'Tomorrow. At four of the clock, St Andrew's church. I shall sit on the second pew in the south side – by the picture of Christ.'

'How do I know you will be there? How do I know you won't bring him with you?'

She laughs, an uneasy, hollow laugh. 'Because he will kill us both if he finds out you have been 'ere enquiring after 'im! Now be gone. I tell you, it's not safe.' She ventures out from behind the bed and towards me. I need no coaxing; I am as glad to leave this place and go to the shelter and safety of my home, as she is to have me gone.

I nod and walk out of her room as quietly and quickly as I can, then down the steep staircase, through the two doors and out into the dark night.

★ ★ ★

As I sit at my dresser going over the details of the night, too awake to go to sleep, too tired to undress, I catch a glimpse of myself in the mirror and recoil at the sight. In the candlelight I see the woman, Eliza, in my own features.

★ ★ ★

It is about seven in the morning as I rise from my bed. I am weary from the events of the previous night but I cannot sleep. My eyes are heavy; they sting with tiredness. I cannot stop thinking about this woman – Eliza. Who is she? Why does she look so much like me? I have recalled as many of her features to mind as I can remember: the curve of her face, the dark brown of her eyes, the curl of her hair. Features similar to my father's and mine, and yet she looks only like me. Could she be his sister? Perhaps she ran away from home – for the love of this man, John, and has been cast off?

I am full of confusion. What do I do? If this is the secret what has it to do with me? The man's words haunt me: 'Then we'll take her'. There was menace in his voice; menace and delight – like the idea had only just struck him and he liked it. He liked it very much. And, of course - he knows where I live! Is this man, even now, watching the house so that he can grab me the moment I leave?

I walk over to the window and peer behind the curtains; the street is empty, or at least it appears to be. I release the curtain quickly. I suddenly feel very cold. I must speak with someone.

I must go to my Uncle; this man must be arrested – and before he thinks again to kidnap me! If I go now, my Uncle is likely to still be at home.

But if I go, what will happen to Eliza? If she is my father's sister, how will she survive if John is hanged? God knows I want this man to pay for murdering my father, but what of Eliza? She will be alone. Perhaps, I can help her – my father is sure to have left some provision for me in his will. Yes, that is it! I shall give her some money to set herself up; she will be financially secure, and maybe one day, when I am older, I shall go out to see her – when my mother can no longer command what I do and where I go.

I put on the clothes I wore the night before, even though they are creased and untidy, and rushing down the stairs, call for the chaise to take me to my Uncle's house.

★ ★ ★

My uncle's house is not far from my own, although today it seems to take forever to reach it. I sit in the chaise twisting the ribbons from my bonnet round and round my fingers until all circulation is lost. I look down at my skirt and try to straighten the creases from it; I wish I had worn a different skirt – I can still smell the putrid decay of the alley on its hems.

Finally, the chaise winds into the driveway. Before it is brought to a standstill, I open the door and jump out almost falling as the gravel slips from under my feet.

I run up the steps to the front door and pull on the doorbell, three maybe four times. I am still panting when the footman opens the door. Pushing him aside, knocking the door from his hand, I rush into my uncle's house, and upstairs into his study.

'Clara!' He puts down his paper as I burst in, and leaps up from his chair. 'What is it my dear? Why are you here at such an early hour?' He stands looking at my dishevelled appearance.

'Uncle! They mean to kidnap me!'

★ ★ ★

My uncle sits me down on the chair next to him, and holding my hand between his, says, 'Clara. Let's start at the beginning.' He looks patiently into my eyes, and I take a deep breath.

'Last night, I went to the Meeting House.'

My uncle starts with shock, his mouth open, about to say something, but I carry on. I shake my head: I must go back further.

'Yesterday,' I pause. 'Yesterday, after I left you at the tearooms, I went to my father's grave. I saw a woman there, putting flowers on his grave. I had never seen her before in my life, but she looked familiar to me. I wanted to speak to her, but she took off before I could say anything. I followed her. I kept my distance so that she did not know it, and then she went in. She went into the Meeting House.' I stop and pause, looking intently at my uncle to make sure he is still listening and has not given me up for some fool. He is listening – and more intently than I would have expected.

'I decided that I would return to the Meeting House last night, after you told me that you were not going to investigate my father's murder any further. I thought this woman may have some idea of why my father had been murdered – who had murdered him.

'I waited until mama was in bed and then I crept out. I waited outside the Meeting House until all the people had left and the lights extinguished, then I went inside – through the back door. I went up the stairs to the servants' quarters and heard a woman – Eliza – arguing with a man. It was the man I had heard arguing with my father the night he died! His name is John, uncle and he admitted to murdering my father!' I pause again to make sure that my uncle has heard the name of my father's murderer, so that he can go and arrest him when I have finished speaking. My uncle looks white and nervous. He nods his head for me to continue.

'They were arguing about trying to get money from us – just as I had heard the man argue with my father. The woman, Eliza, did not want to stay around for him to get the money, but he said it was their right. And then,' I stop: it is too dreadful to repeat, '...then, he said they should kidnap me.'

'I went to leave, as soon as I realised that my life was in danger, but before I could I was discovered! I pretended to be drunk and curled myself into a ball on the floor. Eliza managed to get him away, and then she discovered that I wasn't one of her drunken friends: she knew me.' I look into my uncle's eyes, 'She knew me, uncle – and not just from the graveyard, I am sure.' I pause again, but my uncle sits as still as before. 'She didn't tell me why it was that John wanted to blackmail my father – why he killed him. She said it was too dangerous. She wouldn't say why he wanted to kidnap me. She just said that she would meet me today and explain everything to me.'

I take a deep breath.

'Uncle, this woman – Eliza – she looks like me.' My uncle starts in his seat. 'Is she ... is she... are we related?' He looks down at the rug in front of him and sighs. Then he takes a deep breath and straightens his back.

'Yes, Clara.' He gets up and paces the room. He sighs heavily and then turning towards me, says, 'She is your mother.'

I recoil and let out a small cry. I look at my uncle, stare at him. I search for something to say. I can feel the blood draining from my face. My uncle looks back at me with kindness in his eyes, and walks back towards me again, perching himself on the chaise next to me.

'Your mother... Your mother, Clarissa, could not have a child. We do not know why. After three years of marriage, she remained barren. It did not seem to matter to your father, but it did to her. She wanted a child – desperately. Your father suggested they go to a workhouse and adopt an orphan child, but your mother objected: she wanted your father's child. She was very much in love with him: she didn't think it fair that he should not have his own child to inherit his title just because she was barren. She spoke over and over of him siring a child by another woman – a maid, and then paying the woman for the child. Your father was outraged – and quite rightly so. But your mother insisted and kept on insisting. She ground him down by it. She turned it round on him and accused him of failing her by not providing a child for her to love and nurture. They argued – constantly. Until, one night, in a drunken stupor and after another fight, your father left the house and met Eliza. He laid with her – only the once,' he looks at me as though this will provide me with some consolation, 'and well, you know the result.'

'No! No – uncle, this cannot be true...' I collapse back into my chair. Tears are rolling down my face. To think that my father committed such a sin – my father who I had always looked up to and respected! I want to be out of here. I want to run, to run as far away as I can and never come back!

My uncle takes hold of my hand.

'It was a mistake, Clara. You must not think any less of your father. He was a good man. Even good men may make mistakes when they are pushed – and pushed he was! He was not a saint – no man is. But he was a good man. Do not think ill of him – he thought ill enough of himself. Your father was desperate – he could not believe he had been so weak. He never forgave himself. Unlike your mother – Clarissa. She was delighted. They moved to the country, near to Eliza. Your mother visited her nearly every day. They sent back reports to me of how Clarissa was with child, her condition and then her lying in. Then, a few weeks after you were born, they returned, bringing you with them and raising you as their own.

'It was the undoing of your father; he was never the same after that. He lost his gaiety and sense of humour; he all but locked himself away from society. The only place he visited was the Meeting House. It was the death of your parent's relationship. But Clarissa cared little about it – she had you.'

'But she always seemed to despise me, uncle!'

'Yes – yes. When your hair darkened and you were not the blonde, blue eyed beauty she had wished for; when you started to show your own mind and would not do as she wished you to do…'

'What is to become of me now?' My voice is weak: I can hardly bear to hear myself ask the question, but I must know.

My uncle looks puzzled. 'Will you let him take me?' I falter, my courage gone.

'No, no. You will live with your mother – Clarissa – as normal. You must not speak of this to anyone though, you do understand? I shall speak with your mother and then find this man and arrest him.'

'But uncle, if you do, he will surely tell everyone our secret!'

He pauses. 'I shall find some way of dealing with him,' he says, though it is clear that he has no idea of how.

'Where are you to meet this woman? Eliza?'

'At St Andrew's Church. Four of the noon.'

'You must not go. It may be a trap.'

'No, no, uncle. I cannot believe that. She gave me her word. She was so clear that he should not know. She will not tell him.'

'She may not tell him, but he may find out anyway. It is too dangerous. We cannot risk it. I cannot risk your going there. I shall go instead and bid her be gone. I will tell her that the secret is out and there is no use in trying to extract the money from our family: we shall not pay.'

'Yes, uncle.'

'And you must do as I say from now on.'

'Yes, uncle.' In truth, I am glad to leave it all to someone else now. I have enough to think about when I consider how I am to deal with my mother, Clarissa.

'Now, let us get you home. There is one errand I must do, then I shall speak with your mother.' He takes my hand and putting it under his arm, we leave; I in my chaise and he in his.

★ ★ ★

I am lying on my bed when my uncle calls me to come downstairs and talk with him and my mother. It has been over an hour since I returned from his house, and came straight up to my room: I could not face my mother now that I know who I am. I have worried all the time about her reaction; will she cast me out? Will she curse me for finding out the secret? She cannot surely get rid of me? This is – was – my father's house. He has surely made some provision for me? I am his only heir.

I walk down the familiar stairs to the morning room; stairs I have trodden a thousand times before, but which seem strange to me now. I pause at the door, and knock.

'Clara, my dear!' My uncle walks towards me, his arms outstretched. 'Come and sit down.' He sits me beside my mother; I feel uncomfortable being so close to her. Then he takes his seat opposite to us.

'Clarissa,' he sighs. 'Clara has found out our secret. She knows that her real mother is the woman Eliza who is presently working at the Meeting House.'

My mother shrieks. She looks between my uncle and me trying to figure out whether he is joking; whether to be shocked or pleased. She holds her handkerchief up to her mouth and stares at me.

My uncle coughs. 'Clara, I have some bad news for you.' He pauses. 'I have just been to see my lawyer. I wanted to know his views on your guardianship. As you know, neither your mother, Clarissa here, nor I, are your natural relatives.Your mother was never made your legal guardian when you were born – there was no need to: your father was alive. But now that your father has gone, and what with Eliza around to claim you as her child, I wished to know whether your mother could become your legal guardian. Your father died without making provision for it in his will.' He takes a deep breath.

'My lawyer informs me that there is little your mother, Clarissa, nor I can do to keep you here if it is against Eliza's wishes.' I gasp in disbelief, as does my mother. My uncle reaches inside his pocket and pulls out some papers. 'But I have had my lawyers draw up some papers for Eliza to sign, making us your legal guardians – your mother and I. I shall meet with her this afternoon and make her sign the papers.'

I am so shocked by his words that I cannot take in all that he is saying.

'But what.... what if she refuses to sign?' I ask.

'Then I am afraid that we shall have to let her take you if she wishes...'

'But surely, my father has made some provision for me in his will? Do I not have money or property? Can I not pay them off if that is all they want?'

'No!' My mother cries. She starts from her seat. 'No! We cannot let it happen!' She looks at my uncle, waiting for his agreement. I stare at my mother; I cannot believe that the money means more to her than me; but then, of course, I am not her child. My eyes prick with tears.

'It is true, they will most likely be back for more....' My uncle responds.

'No! No! I will not let it happen! No,' my mother continues, 'she is my child. I will not let her go!' She looks at my Uncle, and before he can even speak says, 'No! Do not say it. Do not say it! She is my child! She always has been and she always will be!' She speaks slowly and deliberately.

I am shocked – delighted - to hear these words – and with such passion!

'Clarissa. She is not your child. She was Henry's child. And now that Henry is gone, if her mother wishes to take her we cannot stand in her way.' My uncle is clear; he appears almost contented.

'No, I will not do it. She cannot have her. I will not allow it. They will have to take me away first! They will have to kill me before I will let her go.'

'Clarissa let us not get over dramatic about it. If Eliza wishes to take Clara with her, we have no right to prevent her from doing it.'

'You want her to go, don't you? You want her to claim Clara and take her away!'

'Clarissa! How can you say such a thing? I am her uncle. I have had the papers drawn up for her to sign!'

'Show me!'

'What?'

'The papers. Show them to me!'

My uncle fumbles in his pocket and hands them over. My mother reads them and nods, then hands them back to my uncle.

'What if Eliza signs them but John still tries to blackmail us?' I ask.

'My lawyers have added a clause: if either one of them tries to blackmail us, or if they speak to any other person of your parentage, John Gotts will immediately be arrested and tried for murder.'

'John Gotts!' I cry. 'When did you find out his name?'

My uncle stops. His face reddens.

'When uncle? When did you find him out?'

He looks away from me.

'Never mind about that!' my mother cries. 'It is you I am concerned about. George, you will make sure she signs them?' my mother asks.

'I will,' he says. His voice is hard; he is beginning to scare me.

'Then she will be safe, won't she George? After Eliza signs the papers, Clara will be safe? Won't she?' She is insistent but not convinced.

He moves away from me, closer to my mother, and taking hold of her elbow, whispers, 'I cannot be sure, Clarissa. You must prepare yourself for that.'

'No!' she screams. 'Then you must find this man and arrest him for murder!'

'And risk our reputation? He will surely speak of Henry's secret! We shall be cast out of all society! We agreed I would not arrest him. Clarissa, we agreed!'

'That was before he threatened to take Clara!' My mother turns on him.

'Clarissa! Think of our reputation!'

My mother laughs but my uncle continues,

'If Clara is kidnapped, it could be the best for us all: Clara will be with her real mother and we shall maintain our reputations. You shall get to keep the house and the money. We shall tell everyone that Clara has been kidnapped. I shall offer to investigate: they will let me do it, being her uncle. I shall find no trace of where she is gone. Over time, people will forget, you will forget and we will be able to stand tall; we will not have been touched by Henry's weakness. I have been able to convince people that Henry's murderer cannot be found, I shall be able to do this.'

I cannot believe what my uncle is saying! I stagger as the words start to make sense in my mind. 'You knew? You knew and yet you have covered it all up? You would rather my father's murderer walk free than risk the family's reputation and money?' And then I laugh at him, hysterically. 'You wish me to live with my father's murderer? You think that is the best thing for me?' I walk over to the window. I had gone to my uncle hoping for protection, but now it appears that he is willing to give me up; even into the hands of my father's murderer! My legs start to give way. I can hear their voices continuing; my mother shouting, my uncle all calmness. But their words become slow and distorted. I stagger but miss the window seat. I fall to the ground hitting my head as I go.

★ ★ ★

The sunlight is fading as I open my eyes. I am lying on my bed again. My head throbs; the slightest movement makes me wince with pain. I lift my hand to my head; but someone is holding onto it: it is my mother.

'You fell and struck your head on the window seat.' She smiles at me, her eyes empty and lost. A tear runs down her face and her smile weakens. She drops her head and I see the tear fall on to my bed covers, darkening the pink of the silk. It spreads into an uneven circle.

I look around the room. My uncle is gone; we are alone. I am glad for it.

'I will never let you go,' my mother whispers as though she can read my thoughts. 'We will go from here, to somewhere where no one will know us, where no-one can find us. We shall live a solitary life, in a small house; perhaps by a stream.' She smiles at me again. It is the most tender smile I have seen since I was a small child.

My mouth is dry and I have difficulty speaking.

'But I am not your child...'

She bows her head again. Her shoulders shake as she sobs silently.

'I have loved you as my own from the moment you were born. You were the child I could not have. You are my husband's child and I have loved you for it.'

'I have irritated you!'

She smiles.

'You were more your father's child than I thought possible. I am sorry I have not been the mother I should have been, but I have loved you. I still love you. I will not let you go, not to him, not to anyone. Please tell me you want to be with me?'

She is fragile now – more fragile than I have ever seen.

'Yes,' I whisper, and feel tears rolling from my eyes onto the pillows.

I look past her and out of the window. The light is fading further.

'What time is it?' I sit up but my temples throb and ache. My mother looks at me in confusion then over to the clock on my mantle piece. 'A quarter past three' she says.

'I must go!' I try to move from the bed but the pounding in my head makes me stop.

'Why? Where must you go to? You are not well!'

I start to climb out of the bed, away from my mother. 'You must not leave the house!' she pleads. 'You are in grave danger!'

'So is she!' I look at my mother and can see in her eyes that she knows who it is I am speaking of.

'I will come with you,' she replies.

★ ★ ★

We ride side by side to St Andrew's Church. I am desperate for this journey to end; frantic that we may not arrive in time to find Eliza – that my uncle will come here first. I am afraid that he may kill her; the words he has spoken today show that he cares only for his own reputation, that he is prepared to anything to leave it intact. If Eliza refuses to sign the papers, who knows what he may do to her?

The sky is darkening as the chaise pulls into the churchyard. Black clouds are gathering above the tower, the leaves are rustling hard in the trees. The clock strikes four as we pull to a stop outside the large wooden gates. My heart sinks when I see another carriage outside the church.

'Uncle is here already!'

My mother steps down from the chaise without saying a word and, hitching up her skirts, runs inside the church.

I follow as quickly as I can but the jogging makes my head hurt even more. I join my mother at the font. She is frantically looking around her. I cannot see Eliza anywhere. I walk further into the church and towards the south transept where the picture of Christ is, where we have arranged to meet. She is not here!

My mother calls out my uncle's name; there is no response. I am afraid. I look from one side of the church to the other, and then I hear footsteps above us, in the bell chamber.

'The roof!' My mother calls and runs towards the bell chamber. She opens the door and starts to go up the steps.

'Mama! No!' I cry, but she has already gone.

I run back to the font and follow her up the winding steps to the top of the tower. There is a cold wind blowing. I can see silhouettes of people against the darkening sky.

'Well, well, well, what 'ave we 'ere then? A right pretty throng!' It is the mocking voice of my father's murderer. I do not need to look at him to see his sarcastic smile. 'Come to snuff out the family's secret, eh? Or do you just want to come straight home wi' me?'

He starts towards me, and I shrink back. My mother stands in front of me.

'Well, well, the doting mother going to protect 'er young? 'Cept she isn't yours is she?'

'John!' Eliza shouts out. 'Leave her be!' She runs over to him but he flings her off like a dirty rag. She falls to the ground.

I stand out from behind my mother. 'I'm not afraid of you!'

He laughs. 'That's what your father said before I cut 'im down'. I lunge towards him; I will strike him down for speaking so ill of my father. But before I know it, he catches hold of me and throws me to the ground.

'Stop!' Eliza cries. 'There's no need for this John. I'll sign the papers; she can stay with her family. We're not her family; she's been brought up well. An' so she should. She should 'ave the best; she's a lady.' To my surprise my uncle walks towards her with the papers.

'Get off wi' yer!' John shouts and hitting out at my uncle knocks him to the ground. Then he turns and grabs hold of my hands and drags me to my feet.

'Leave her!' It is Eliza's voice again. She has climbed onto one of the four turrets which stand at the corners of the bell tower. Her body and her feet are facing outwards towards the edge. She turns her face towards us, looking over her shoulder.

'Don't be such a fool, woman.'

'I'll do it, John. You just try me! Leave her be, you hear me! It's over, can't you see? We can't win!'

'She's our property and I'll be damned if we leave 'er behind.' He starts towards me again, and as he does my mother lets out a piercing shriek. There is a thud and Eliza is gone.

John rushes to the edge of the tower and looking over lets out a long, low scream; like an animal, mortally wounded. Then he turns and with a face as a dark as the clouds, he starts towards me.

'This is your doing!'

'Keep away!' My uncle shouts, he is holding a pistol in his hand. 'Away or I'll shoot!'

John ignores him and continues towards me.

A shot rings out and John staggers backwards, his face alight as though he has just woken from a dream. He looks down at his chest, flowing with blood, then staggers over to the edge of the tower and leans over until he, too, topples.

I hold my breath and grab hold of the wall to steady myself. My mother has collapsed onto the floor. She is crying hysterically. On the ground below, people are starting to gather around the two bodies.

'Quickly!' My uncle shouts. 'Go downstairs and say nothing.' He picks my mother up from off the floor.

We do as we are bid, walking slowly and uneasily down the steps. The ringing of the pistol is still fresh in my ears.

'Sit on the pews and pray!' he orders. 'I'll be back in a minute!' Then he leaves us and goes outside.

★ ★ ★

Today is the inquest into the deaths of Eliza and John Gotts. I shall not be called as a witness on account of being a lady. My uncle, being constable, and having witnessed the deaths, will tell all.

It has been two weeks since John and Eliza came by their deaths and we have not seen my uncle at all during this time.

My mother, or should I say, my adoptive mother, has been the sweetest I have ever known her; patient beyond recognition. She has never once sighed with irritation as she has unpicked my embroidery and shown me, again, how to sew neatly. And I, well, I am full of admiration for her – she has chosen me over her reputation, a child who is not even her own flesh and blood.

'All rise!'

The coroner enters. He is a stout man with greying hair and large eyebrows. He wears small round spectacles on the end of his nose and holds his pocket watch in his hand as he walks to his chair. The chair is a little too high for him and he stands on tiptoe as he lifts himself onto it and shuffles backwards.

He clears his throat.

'Gentlemen of the Jury. I sit today to determine the circumstances surrounding the deaths of these two unfortunate persons, Eliza Gotts, born on the 22nd February 1794 and John Gotts born on the 19th March 1786. Eliza Gotts was aged 37 at the time of her death on the 23rd July 1831 and John Gotts aged 45 years at the time of his death on the same date.

'I have before me the sworn evidence of Dr William Walker, a medical person who testifies that the cause of death of Eliza Gotts was from multiple injuries caused by a fall from a great height, and that John Gott died from a single gunshot wound to his chest. Both bodies were found at the bottom of the tower at St Andrew's church in the parish of Hempstead in the county of Norfolk.

'It is for you, the Jurors, to decide how these people came by their deaths; whether it be a killing – lawful or unlawful – or suicide.

'You will now hear the evidence of Sir George Felton, constable of the Parish of Hempstead.'

The coroner nods and my uncle takes the stand. After swearing the oath he continues, 'On the 23rd day of July, 1831, I had been in pursuit of the man John Gotts, having suspected him of the murder of Sir Henry Bedingfield.'

'During the course of my investigation, it came to my attention that on the evening of the 11th June 1831, the deceased John Gotts was seen to be abusing a young woman, within the precincts of the Meeting House. Sir Henry, it appears, went to the woman's aid whereupon the deceased set upon him. This man, John Gotts, was seized by other members of the establishment and thrown out. It appears that although John Gotts was instructed not to return, he did indeed do so, and during that time killed Sir Henry on account of his heroic and gentlemanly actions.

I let out a small gasp; how could my uncle know so much and until now, say so little? My mother takes hold of my hand and squeezes it. I look up at her but she keeps her eyes fast upon my uncle. No one else has heard my outburst and so my uncle continues.

'It was on the 23rd July 1831, that I set out to arrest the said John Gotts for the murder of Sir Henry Bedingfield, having lain in wait for him on numerous occasions. In attempting to apprehend the scoundrel, he took flight. I followed him in my carriage to St Andrew's church. I saw him enter the church, and though it was the House of God, felt compelled nevertheless to follow him. I had on my person, for my own protection, a pistol. Once within the church, I confronted the deceased and asked him to come quietly. He threw innumerable profanities at me – which I will not repeat, there being many ladies present...' He pauses to look at the coroner who nods his head in disgusted agreement, '...whereupon I informed him that he was to be arrested for murder. After issuing more profanities, he said that I would never take him alive and fled to the church tower. I followed him up the steps, not once thinking of my own safety.

'As I entered onto the roof, the vagabond grabbed hold of my collars and tried to throw me down the very steps I had just climbed. I managed to straighten myself and fought him off. I produced my pistol and explained to the deceased that I would not hesitate to use it if he came at me again. He, however, did not heed my words and like a man possessed lurched towards me whereupon I discharged a single bullet, the force of which threw him backwards and over the edge of the turret. It was only at this time that I became aware of the woman Eliza Gott's presence. She shrieked and rushed over to where he had fallen, and upon seeing his body on the ground, climbed onto the turret and flung herself over saying that she could not live without him.'

I let out a small cry; the man is lying! My uncle is lying! I sit forward in my chair not knowing whether to speak out or not. The room is as silent as it had been when my uncle gave his evidence, only now, heads are turned in my direction. My mother, who has kept hold of my hand throughout, squeezes it again, but remains composed, her eyes fixed upon my uncle. I immediately avert my eyes and bite my lip. My mind is racing. My uncle is saving us; me, my family, our name. But he is lying! And to a court! I have the chance to rectify it; to tell the truth. Should I speak up? Me, an orphan, with only my father's wife and her brother to look after me, until I reach the age of maturity or marry. And who will marry me, if they learn of the truth – of my true parentage?

But how can I live with this man? This man who will stop at nothing to maintain his reputation? In truth, I am afraid of my uncle – he has killed and is now lying about it. What will he do to me if I speak up? He will not be put away for lying in a court of law – and he did kill in self defence; I saw that and so did my mother. Unless, of course, I lie. I could tell the court that my uncle killed in cold blood: that he could have arrested the man, but instead killed him for the revenge of my father. My mother will back me up – she is as frightened of him as I am, now that we both know that he is capable of killing someone.

But what am I thinking? There is every chance that she may not! And what will happen to me then? I shall have to live with Clarissa and my uncle, and both will know how I was prepared to see my uncle hang for murder.

'Yes, my dear? Do you have something to say?' The coroner interrupts my thoughts. I look up at him, his eyes are kind and searching.

I look at him for a moment, trying to decide what to do. And then I stand. My mother lets out a gasp and drops my hand. She looks up at me, puzzled.

I open my mouth but no words come out. I stand, like a fool, twisting the cords on my purse. I can feel my uncle stare but I do not look at him.

'I … I…'

'Yes?' The coroner's voice is gentle.

Still I cannot speak a word; I just look at him while tears stream down my face. I look at him. My legs are shaking. I feel quite sick. I open my mouth,

'I am sorry', I whisper. This is all I can say!

'Of course, my child. I am sorry you have had to hear all of this. Your father was a brave man; a well respected man. A man to be proud of. Please, feel free to leave.'

I turn and walk slowly out of the room, all eyes upon me. 'I'm sorry,' I repeat. 'I am sorry, Papa.'

And so I walk out and face a future full of lies. I am as inextricably bound up in all of this as my mother and uncle. I walk out of the building and down the street towards my home. Down the street, and past the Meeting House.

Kelvin I. Jones

Kelvin I. Jones is the author of numerous books about
Sherlock Holmes and his creator, Conan Doyle and has
written widely in the fields of supernatural fiction and
crime fiction, his most recent creation being the Cornish
detective, John Bottrell, who first made his appearance in
Stone Dead (2006) and who subsequently appeared in
Witch Jar and Flowers of Evil (2008). He is a creative
writing tutor for the UEA and lives in Aylsham with his
wife Debbie, and two elderly cats.

Kelvin I. Jones

Kett's Heights
- Kelvin I. Jones -

On the morning of June 22nd 1958, the body of Mrs Maria Leonard was discovered in a wooded enclosure on Kett's Heights, a high hill overlooking the city of Norwich. She was naked and her throat had been slashed. The person who made this discovery, a middle aged neighbour, telephoned the police, then sat down on a seat in her adjacent garden, shocked into inaction.

The apparently motiveless murder of Mrs Leonard, an artist's wife who lived nearby at The Cedars, soon made headline news.

Even though it happened over fifty years ago, the events of that summer day are engraved on my mind. I was a child at the time and recalled nothing of what took place. For my father, the matter was a closed book, a terrible event which he kept locked from view. When I questioned him about it years later, he would fall silent and simply look away. Then, at the age of 59, he suffered a stroke, which rendered him voiceless.

I knew then that my mother's death was unlikely to be solved unless I alone unravelled the mystery.

It wasn't until the January of 2006 that I returned to The Cedars. A tall, limestone villa erected by a rich Norfolk wool merchant in the 1850's, it had been the family home for most of my father's lifetime. He had seen it whilst on a sketching holiday way back in the early 50's, shortly after he had met Maria, and had fallen in love with its Grecian pillars, gothic windows and incongruous Dutch style gable ends. At that time the place had fallen into disrepair. The garden was overgrown, several of the bigger trees had fallen and the wall which separated the grounds from Kett's Heights itself had started to crumble.

In 1952, my father married Maria at the Norwich registry office and the couple moved in. A team of their friends helped renovate the place, most of them fellow artists who had been at the Slade with my mother. They painted the walls, scoured antique shops for furniture, cleared the garden of weeds and helped shore up the perimeter wall. Slowly but surely order was restored. Then, in the following summer, I was born.

I retain fleeting memories of my mother: her long, blonde hair, worn to the waist, her startling green eyes, one darker than the other; her bohemian clothes, her soft voice and her gentleness. What I did not know as a child, growing up in that sprawling mansion, was her involvement in occult matters. That knowledge was only granted to me years later. By that time I was living in New York, trying, rather unsuccessfully, to earn a crust as a freelance journalist.

It was a freezing November night. I'd accepted an invitation from a female friend of mine to attend a talk in Brooklyn about an organisation called the Golden Dawn. At the time I knew nothing about The Golden Dawn. I only attended the meeting because my companion was both attractive and, I suspect, eager to see more of me without making it blatantly obvious.

The meeting was held in a dingy hall belonging to the Freemasons just off 47th Precinct. There were few people in the audience that night. The speaker, a tall, ascetic man in his 60's, gave a rambling talk about the history and origins of this organisation, mentioning Aleister Crowley, W.B. Yeats and several other prominent figures during the 1890's. He showed a series of slides to illustrate his talk. When he got to talking about the 1940's, he threw up a slide of a group photo taken on a summer expedition to Cambridgeshire. There, in the background, unmistakeably, was my mother. I could tell it was her from the style of the hair, the long, wistful face and those eyes I remembered from my childhood.

After the talk was concluded, I quizzed the speaker about the photo and he promised to send me a copy of it. It was only some while afterwards that I realised the man she was standing next to was my father's old friend, Robert Spender, who had been a frequent visitor to The Cedars when I was a child.

And that, for the time being, was the end of the matter. In the following months, I read several books about the history of The Golden Dawn but found no further reference to either my mother or Robert Spender. And it was no good asking my father about this episode in my mother's life. He had been dead for nearly ten years.

I arrived at The Cedars early in January 2006. It had been freezing cold in New York, but here the winter was merely a grey blanket of murk and mist with no snow. Kett's Heights is a high prominence overlooking the city. On a fine day you can see the great cathedral with its towering spire and the sweep of the city streets to the flat lands beyond, but today nothing was visible save for the dim glow of street lamps, triggered by the lack of natural daylight. I got the taxi to drop me just below the Heights and, case in hand, walked the remaining distance up the narrow footpath, between ancient oaks and ash trees, heavy with dripping branches, until I reached the remains of St Michael's Chapel. The Heights were much overgrown, more so than I remembered in childhood. Where once had been a grove of yew trees set on a well-trimmed lawn now gave way to briar. Over all this was the damp, fetid stench of vegetation. Local youths had also used the place for night time drinking sessions, it seemed, for the area was strewn with empty lager cans, cigarette packets and used condoms.

I pushed through almost head high brambles into the interior of the ruined chapel. The walls, though lichen coated, were still intact and the altar where they had found my mother all those years ago was still there, though covered in a black fungus. There was a silent, oppressive feel to the place which made me feel slightly uneasy and I did not linger but made my way along the adjoining path to The Cedars.

When I reached the stuccoed portico I found a frail figure waiting for me. It was Mrs Beddoes, the resident of the flat in the eastern wing of the house. Mrs Beddoes had been a friend of my mother's. When my father had purchased The Cedars all those years ago, he had been hard pressed to pay the mortgage and Mrs Beddoes had provided a solution to the problem. Agnes Beddoes was a war widow who, in exchange for a cheap rent, offered her services as an unofficial caretaker of the property on those occasions when my parents went touring in America and Europe.

She waved at me. Her once luxurious auburn hair was now quite white and she was supporting her emaciated frame with a stick. Still, it was good to see a familiar face.

"You'll find the house in a bit of a state," she warned, as we entered the hallway. She was right. The once beautiful stuccoed ceilings were stained brown with damp and paper was peeling from the walls. We passed into the lounge where furniture lay encased in dust sheets. Everywhere there was the smell of damp.

"Some of this stuff will have to go," I said. "The damp's done for it. What this place needs is central heating." Mrs Beddoes agreed.

The installation of the oil fired central heating system absorbed the rest of my meagre savings, but when the job was completed it made such a difference to the eight bedrooms and seven other rooms. I even put heating into Mrs Beddoes' flat, for which she was truly grateful. However, by February, I had no money and I needed a job. As luck would have it, I saw a position in the local paper as a manager of an art gallery. I applied for the job and was interviewed by a tall brunette called Diana, the owner of the gallery. It was shortly after I started work at the gallery that we became lovers.

It was a whirlwind romance. Diana was strong minded and intelligent yet underneath all that confidence and strength lay a curious vulnerability and sensitivity – qualities which made her an ideal gallery owner. She was also, like me, looking for a long term relationship, her previous marriage having ended in disaster.

Diana moved into The Cedars in the May of that same year. The place was still in much the same mess as I hade encountered it on my arrival save for an efficient central heating system and some new furniture.

Diana soon made an impact on our new home. Off came the stained wallpaper, on went subtle shades of emulsion paint. The house acquired new furniture a la mode: potted plants and rugs from Afghanistan covered the newly sanded and polished floorboards. I had never thought such a transformation possible. And when the house was complete, we set to task on the wilderness of the garden.

It was while we were cutting down the shoulder high hogweed that we discovered the stone sculpture. Suddenly the scythe I'd been using hit something, making my forearm judder. I swore, then crouched down and peered into the undergrowth. A dark figure looked back at me from the semi-darkness. I pulled it out and cleared away the earth from the surface of the object. It was a squat - bodied carving with a bulbous head. Blank eyed and with thin lips, it appeared to have been carved from granite. There was a grim, primitive suggestion to the face which indicated the sculpture was of great antiquity. I showed it to Diana who immediately recoiled at my discovery.

"What an ugly thing ! Who could have buried it there?"

"It was only just under the surface. Looks as if someone must have chucked it out some while back. Maybe when my father was doing the renovations to the house."

"Well, it's hideous whatever it is. Puts me in mind of the Easter Island carvings."

"I wonder if it's worth anything? Maybe we should take it to Max at the museum."

Max was Diana's friend, a conservator by profession who had worked for some years at the Ashmolean Museum in Oxford. We wrapped up the sculpture, boxed it, then presented it to him in his office at the museum.

"It's quite a find," he remarked after a considered pause. "Where did you say you found it?"

We explained.

"It's Celtic, pre-Christian. There are dozens like it which have been discovered at various sites round Britain. But this one is usually associated with the north of England. It's a kind of votive offering – an image of the god Maponus."

"Maponus?"

"An ancient Celtic god. He was associated with thresholds and especially the gateway to the underworld. He was the son of Mab or Modron, the great mother goddess. The Romans claimed that when they came to Britain in 46 AD they found Druids worshipping in sacred groves."

"I've read about that."

"Well, this little fellow represents one of the gods they worshipped – and made sacrificial offerings to, of course."

"Human sacrifices?"

"Maybe and maybe not. Some classical writers thought so, of course."

"The wicker man and all that?"

"Perhaps. We do know that some of the northern European tribes practised human sacrifice because we have archaeological evidence to that effect. And then of course there are the peat bog burials. They were Celtic," he added. It was clear that Max was warming to his subject.

"The peat bog burials?"

"You've heard of Pete Marsh, a body uncovered in a peat bog many years ago?"

"Vaguely."

"He was ritually murdered. Given a good meal, some sort of intoxicating substance thrown in, then garrotted, pole axed and drowned in a lake. Probably as an offering to the gods."

"Charming people, the Celts."

We left the museum at around four and dropped into a small café near the rail station. Diana had been deadly quiet all the while Max had been talking about the head.

"What's up?"

"All that business about the sculpture, that's what," she said in a low voice. "It's very odd."

"What is?"

"My dream last night."

"What about it?"

"When I woke up I remembered only fragments of it but when Max was talking it started to come back to me."

She told me about the dream. By the time she'd finished, my coffee was stone cold.

She'd dreamt she was in the ruined chapel – only the chapel wasn't a ruin. It had a roof and stained glass windows and the interior was lit by tall, glittering candles. There was a figure dressed in a black cassock, standing by the high altar, but instead of a cross, there was a goat's head mounted on a long pole. There were several other people in the chapel, dressed in long white robes, and she was one of them. They were chanting something, possibly in Latin. As they approached the altar, one of the company pushed her onto her knees. When she looked up, she found herself staring not at the goat's head but at the granite sculpture we'd found in the grounds. At that point the priest turned and lowered a silver chalice as if giving her communion, but when she leaned forward to taste the liquid it had the warmth and redness of blood. That was all she could remember.

"Probably a memory of some horror film you once watched," I suggested.

"I don't watch horror movies," she replied. Momentarily, I had forgotten that Diana had been raised in America. Sometimes I found that made a difference. Although she was bold, energetic and outspoken, she also possessed a vulnerability and at times slight paranoia.

We made our way back to Norwich and got to the gallery by mid afternoon. We spent the rest of the day hanging the new exhibition, a collection of post expressionist paintings by a German artist. The dark themes of the paintings did not help to dispel Diana's mood, so I was glad when six o'clock finally came round and we could make our way back up to Kett's Heights. As we walked in silence, I remembered what my father had told me about the history of the place. Kett had been a farmer during the middle ages and had raised a crowd some two thousand strong as a protest against the King's policy of enclosures. He'd rampaged through the city, attacking government officials and their houses. When the militia finally caught up with him they'd fought down by the river. Then Kett's men had been driven up the hill, finally taking refuge on the Heights, where many of them were subsequently slaughtered. However, before their defeat, they set fire to the chantry as a protest against the wealth and complicity of the church. Kett himself had been hung, drawn and quartered. No wonder was it, I thought, that the Heights had such a powerful and brooding atmosphere. I decided I would not tell Diana about the history of the place. Maybe the Maponus head had some strange mythic potency which she had tuned into subconsciously. Who could say? Anyway, it was out the way now. That's all that mattered.

That evening we dined on roast beef and drank a deal too much red wine. Then we made passionate love together. Diana seemed to really need me that night and the vulnerability I had seen in her earlier had intensified. I drifted off in her arms and soon fell into a deep, wine induced sleep. When I awoke, I recalled a dream of startling clarity. Normally I do not recall my dreams or I remember vague snatches of them but on this particular morning the memory was fresh, the recall film-like in its sharpness.

It was the summer I went away to boarding school in Suffolk. I remembered that summer very well because it had been one of the hottest on record. Yet in the dream I wasn't at boarding school at all. I was here at The Cedars. And although I was in the house, nobody seemed to notice me. I was, it seems, an invisible observer.

My father and Robert Spender were sitting in the study, talking animatedly, but I could only catch snatches of their conversation. Something about "midsummer solstice" and "the moon" was all I could glean. They were sitting at a long table laden with books. I can see Robert Spender's face with great clarity. He had been a frequent visitor to The Cedars but was not well liked by my mother as I recall. A tall, dark haired man with a widow's peak and bushy eyebrows, he had penetrating eyes that were a deep brown and his nose was hawk like. By the way he talked to my father I gained the impression that he had some hold over him and although I could not hear much of what he was saying, he was speaking in a forceful manner, leaning over the table every so often and using his hands to demonstrate his point. At the end of the conversation I heard my father say: "But she will not do it of her own free will." And then came the reply: "Then by force."

When I woke it was getting light and the room was intensely cold. I switched on the side lamp and sat thinking for a while, listening to the sound of Diana's breathing. Was it a dream or a confused memory? I knew that in the dreamscape time often became confused and compressed. Perhaps there were two separate memories here which had been combined. What was it that the two men had been discussing so earnestly? I began thinking about "uncle Bob", as my father described him to me. He had been a regular visitor to the house, usually arriving unannounced, then being closeted with my father for hours at a time. And I recalled my mother's unease with this tall, imposing figure. She referred to him not as "uncle Bob", but as "that man Spender" and I remembered that he was never a topic of conversation between my parents.

Yet again I began thinking about the photograph I had seen in New York. Clearly my mother and father had known Spender for a number of years in connection with the Golden Dawn. Just what was the nature of that connection and why didn't my mother like him?

The next morning I didn't go into the gallery since it was my morning off. Normally I would have devoted the time to my painting but this particular morning I decided to take advantage of the new broadband facility we'd had installed. I googled Robert Spender. It turned out Spender's father, Henry, had been a leading light in the Golden Dawn in the 1900's and was connected with Aleister Crowley, the notorious magician, having attended his circle on the island of Cefalu shortly before the authorities threw Crowley out. Henry Spender was also a leading freemason in his time and worth a small fortune, being the heir to a mustard firm. His son took on the mustard - manufacturing dynasty when his father died in 1948. However, I could find out little about Robert Spender apart from his being educated at Eton and Oxford where he obtained a degree in anthropology and the fact that he had written two obscure monographs, one on Celtic Pagan Religion, the other on the Cult of Mithras. A quick search of the second hand books sites soon yielded a copy of each monograph which I immediately ordered.

The following day I had to go to London on business and didn't arrive back until late that same evening. By the time the train got into Norwich station a dense fog had risen and as I made my way over the bridge great swathes of mist had enveloped the buildings, leaving the street lamps as points of light in a white sea. I climbed up to Kett's Heights, aware of the utter silence of my surroundings. When I finally reached The Cedars, I found Diana sitting in a chair in the lounge in her dressing gown. She was staring fixedly at the fireplace and seemed hardly to notice my entrance.

"What's up?" I asked. "Didn't you hear me come in?"

"Couldn't sleep," she said, her voice remote and tremulous. "Listen. Can't you hear them?"

"Hear who?"

"The voices."

I listened. I could hear nothing. Then she told me what had happened. She had gone to bed early after experiencing a migraine. Around 11 pm she had been woken by the sound of voices. At first she thought they were in the house but when she went downstairs she realised they were coming from the direction of the old chapel, which lies adjacent to the garden wall of The Cedars. She put on her clothes and went to investigate, but when she got into the garden she heard nothing. Returning to the house, she heard them again, one a man's voice, the other a woman's.

She said the woman sounded distressed, frightened. The man's voice was coaxing, persuasive. I made Diana a hot milk, laced with whisky, and we both went to bed. Maybe in the morning, I thought, things would seem clearer.

But things were not clearer in the morning. Diana rose, pale and tired, still convinced about the voices. She seemed utterly depressed and fatigued, quite unlike her usual self. I suggested she take the morning off and that I open the gallery.

By the Friday of that same week she seemed much improved. On that same morning a package arrived containing the two books I'd ordered. That evening I dipped into "Celtic Pagan Religion", which turned out to be a mish-mash of fact and fantasy. The author set out to establish the credentials for a religion of the Celts. Since most of the historical evidence for these far spread tribes came from classical authors, he appeared to rely largely on supposition and a vivid imagination to fill in the missing gaps. There was much discussion about human sacrifices and offerings to the gods and the author inclined to the view that since such concepts were commonly held to be valid in the classical world, then why should they not still hold true ? I had begun to tire of this confused ramble when I spotted an entry under the heading: "Celtic Gods."

"Maponus", the text ran, otherwise known as Maponos, figures in the mabinogi of Culhwch. He was also known by his mother's name, Mabon Yab Modron, "Son, son of Mother." Dedications to this god occur in Northumberland, Cumberland and Norfolk. He is associated with hunting and also with the threshold between the living and the dead. Many of the places dedicated to Maponus were hill top shrines or nemetons as the Romans called them – groves of oak trees. In Britain especially these sites were later Christianised and rededicated to St Michael, the Archangel and dragon slayer, a small church or chapel being erected.

In north west Normandy two shrines were discovered in the early 19th Century, dedicated to the god. Both were tomb-like structures which, on excavation, yielded numerous skulls and bones. The Roman writer Tacitus refers to the discovery of a wooded grove in north eastern Germany dedicated to Malponius in the following terms:

'On entering the grove of oak trees the legionaries stood in horror and would go no further. Hanging from the boughs of trees were the severed limbs of men, women and children and, before them, cut from the rock, was a deep basin filled with blood, evidence of their terrible barbarity. The order was given to cut down the trees and bury what remained of the corpses.'

I decided that, under the circumstances, it would be better not to tell Diana about the entry in Spender's book.

The following day dawned bright and warm and there was a suggestion of spring in the air. I decided that, since I had the morning off from the gallery, I would spend the morning sketching on Kett's Heights, joining Diana later in town for lunch. Making my way down the footpath, I soon gained access to the grove and the ruined chapel and settled down on a bench with pencils and a sketchpad. A bright morning sun had risen in the east and was shining directly at me, so that I found myself constantly shielding my eyes with my free hand. After about an hour's sketching, I started to feel drowsy, and, putting my pencil aside, I lay back and drifted off, listening to the bird song and the sound of the wind in the beeches.

Some while later I awoke with a start to find a tall, hooded youth standing staring at me. He said nothing but I found his stillness and silence threatening.

"Yes ?" I said. "Can I help you ?"

I stared at his pale face. He was thin and gaunt and his flesh was covered with acne. He didn't reply but simply turned and walked away in the direction of the steps. The event unnerved me, though I was unable to say why. He had done nothing to threaten me, he hadn't even spoken to me. Maybe he was just curious, I told myself. He must have seen me asleep on the bench, noted the sketchpad, realised I was an artist, probably wondered what I was doing there. That was it. It was an innocuous event after all and I was foolish to feel the way I did. Yet there was something about the way he'd stood and looked at me which put my nerves on edge. It was as if I had intruded into his territory. This was nonsense, I told myself. The Heights was a public place where anyone might wander at will. Yet public spaces had their dangers. Only last week a young woman had been stabbed in a park in Norwich near the city centre. She had only just survived the attack. The crime was apparently motiveless. How foolish of me to have fallen asleep like that. I mustn't let it happen again. And there was something more, too, a sense of menace about the Heights which perhaps I'd failed to comprehend. Maybe it was true what the ancients believed about places. That they each have their genius loci and that what happens there, whether it be joy or tragedy, leaves an indelible mark on that location. What else could explain the lingering power of the haunted house on the mind of the sensitive ?

I returned to the house, feeling shaken after my experience, then went into Norwich where I joined Diana for lunch. Once again I decided not to tell her about what had happened to me. But in a sense nothing had happened.

Spring turned to summer. The gallery began to prosper and I found that my time was increasingly occupied with business. As time went on, Diana seemed to grow more relaxed in the house and even took to gardening. As we cleared the remaining areas of waste land that had once formed the perimeter of my father's garden, more pieces of statuary and stonework came to light. Some of the large pieces appeared to come originally from the chapel and, on examination, we found sections of the garden wall had pieces of limestone inset, as if the builder of the house had robbed the chapel remains. I recalled reading somewhere about old churches being built on places of pagan worship. When the buildings of the New Religion appeared in England the building blocks of ancient tombs were often used as part of the fabric of churches.

When summer came that fateful year it was a heat wave. On midsummer's eve I had been on a trip to London to help organise a joint exhibition. Returning home late to Norwich, I ate with Diana, then we decided to enjoy the cool of the evening on Kett's Heights. As we passed down the narrow footpath, we thought we could hear voices from the inside of the ruined chapel.

"Sounds like youths," I said. As we pushed our way through some tall hawthorn bushes at the eastern end, we saw a group of six youths standing around the ruined altar. There, stretched out on the flat stone, was a young girl with short blonde hair. She was quite naked and crouched forwards, her head lying in folded arms. On top of her was a lean, muscular youth, also naked, moving back and forth with quick, powerful strokes. The six youths, who were clearly drunk, cheered and clapped at the spectacle as if they were at a football match and the tallest of them was taking photos of the event with his mobile phone. I pulled at Diana's arm, sensing danger, but she shouted something at them. Immediately the dark youth spun round, glaring at us. He swore, then lurched over to Diana and pulled her by the hair towards the altar where the two youths by now had consummated their lust.

"You're next !" he shouted and his audience burst into applause. I moved forwards to try and stop the madness but I wasn't quick enough for one of them who produced a long bladed knife and lunged at me. A sharp searing pain shot up my arm.

When I looked again I could see he had cut me badly. Two of the youths were now dragging Diana onto the altar and a third had torn away her cotton dress. I struggled to get up but already I was losing consciousness.

Some while later I stirred. I was lying in a pool of blood. The youths had gone. Diana was crouched by the altar, moaning to herself. I found my mobile and called the emergency services.

I was able to give the police a detailed description of two of the youths. Fortunately, the gang were known to them. Only the previous evening they'd raided a local off licence and severely beaten the manager and his colleague. Diana and I attended a line up and had no difficulty in identifying the rapist and his accomplice. Because they were both under age they received only short custodial sentences.

About a month after the incident Diana left me. The traumatic nature of her ordeal, the house, the place itself, these were all contributory factors in our split up. Yet in some ways we had also grown increasingly apart during the year we had lived at The Cedars.

Is it true that places can have a powerful effect on the way we think and act ? I believe it is possible. The past is a mysterious country which lays claim to us in many ways, some of which we are not even able to comprehend. This was so with Kett's Heights.

After Diana left me I became severely depressed. I rarely left the place and when I did, I seldom ventured down into the city. I took to ignoring the summons of the phone and stopped replying to emails. I kept thinking that somewhere in the house I would find a clue to the mystery of my mother's death but I had no idea where to look.

Then, one day in September, the solution presented itself to me. I had been up in the attic, trying to clear space for some of my art materials and paintings. In a corner, among a pile of faded books and papers, I found a tin box bearing the letters JL – my father's initials. I took the box downstairs and prised open the lid. Inside were several documents relating to the Golden Dawn, a collection of photos and diaries spanning the years 1940 – 1962. I began looking through the photos. There were some of my mother and father on holiday by the sea. Probably Kings Lynn I thought. Others were group shots showing seven people whom I didn't recognise with my mother and father outside The Cedars on the lawns.

One in particular caught my eye. It showed Robert Spender, the man who had always been something of a mystery to me. He was standing next to my mother, one arm around her shoulder. The photo, which was clearer than the one I had seen in New York, showed a tall, lean faced man with long jet black hair and penetrating eyes. What influence did this man have over my parents, I wondered? And why had my father never talked about him to me?

I made myself a coffee and settled down to read the diaries. Much of it was mundane stuff but when I got to he mid 1950's, Robert Spender's name increasingly made an appearance. From the way my father wrote about him it appeared he was deeply respected by both my parents. Phrases such as "Robert's knowledge of the occult is profound" and "I have much to learn from this wisest of men" gave me the impression that for my father Spender was some sort of guru.

Then, in the February of 1958, the entries began to lengthen and become more intense. Clearly my father had become obsessed by the notion of propitiation or sacrifice to the gods. In one long entry for March 17, he had written:

The notion of sacrifice was widely held and acknowledged by the ancients. The Romans performed animal sacrifices and the Celts most probably offered human kinds to their ubiquitous gods and goddesses. When an offering is made to a deity, the magus becomes empowered by a current of energy which springs from the Divine Source. The gates of perception are then opened. Most ancient rituals of this sort involved the imbibing of hallucinatory substances to achieve heightened awareness. Robert has been educating both of us in this area and we have already glimpsed through the shadowy veil a world which is more glorious and exalted than our own. He is helping me to prepare for The Great Work. Maria is ready and prepared. Indeed, she anticipated the day of The Ritual with growing excitement. Yet we must be careful. Each detail of the Ritual must be precisely observed, for if it is not, all chaos will be loosed. At present we are both fasting in order to purify our bodies.

I read on. Then, in the entry for June 21, I read this:

The midsummer solstice is finally here. Maria is very excited and I confess so am I. Everything is now prepared. Robert will be here later and then we shall prepare. He will be bringing mescaline to aid us in our task. The little stone statues of Maponus which we found buried in the ruins of the old chapel will be placed on the summit of the hill and when the sun reaches its lowest point, we shall begin The Ritual.

After this there were no more references to rituals or Spender save for one comment under the entry for July 1st 1958.

Robert has left. He has been of great solace to me. Yet all his kind words will never bring back Maria. God forgive me. What have I done ?

And that was an end to the matter. Robert Spender, I subsequently discovered, died in a nursing home in Great Yarmouth a year after I sold The Cedars, so I never got the chance to interrogate him. But then what would he have told me? That he and my father had discovered an ancient statue in the grounds of a chapel and used it as part of some bizarre ritual involving drugs and human sacrifice? Had they really intended to kill my mother as part of some horrific sex rite? Who knows? The participants of The Great Work are now long dead but the place remains.

I revisited Kett's Heights last summer and stood in the ruined chapel, trying to make sense of it all. The sense of foreboding I had felt there before still lingered. Can it be that some places are forever imbued by the pattern of past events? I believe it to be true as much as I believe that what happened to Diana and myself was not purely coincidental but triggered by the dark deeds which emanated from that ancient place. And there is truth in the notion that, although we may have forgotten the old gods, they are not dead but merely sleeping.

And if we awaken them, we do so at our peril.

Kelvin I. Jones

Melanie Keast

I'm fast approaching sixty and have a long suffering
husband, a mother in an annexe, two daughters, two
grandchildren, three dogs, a horse, a geriatric cat and an
unfulfilled ambition - to have a book published.
In 1966, whilst hiding from a hockey lesson at school and
holed up with a transistor radio, I heard The Beatles sing
'Paperback Writer'. With the clarity that eluded me in my
lessons I realised I wanted to pen a novel and see it on the
shelves in Smiths - I don't remember Waterstones being
around then. However youth got in the way, or rather
several youths and I didn't get creative until the pen went
out of fashion and the computer took over. It's taken me a
helluva long time to get into print and I still haven't written
that book, let alone got it published, but God willing, there
still may be time!

Melanie Keast

The Final Straw
- Melanie Keast -

O nly half of the back wheels of the car were visible above the water, the rest was hidden below the opaque surface. Two arches of black rubber like the Loch Ness monster's humps. Everything was quite calm again, the spreading stain of oil polishing the glassy water. Only an occasional bubble broke the surface, releasing the horror below with an audible pop. The car had careered off the lane and flipped onto its back before hurtling into the cold embrace of the lake. The water had swallowed the offering easily, hissing and belching until it was covered, the ever widening ripples butting the bank.

All except for the crescents of tyres. Rubber half moons marking where someone had died.

★ ★ ★

His day had started badly.

He'd overslept and as a result missed his train and had to drive all the way to his office. The traffic had been ponderously slow; the lights always against him and the car park predictably full. Bill Donahue was angry.

He arrived at his desk to find a terse note from his boss reminding him that he'd missed the early morning meeting and that he was expected in his office at his earliest convenience. He could already feel a familiar pain beginning to throb behind his eyes. His boss could wait, he needed coffee. He signalled to his secretary and within seconds she'd delivered his first caffeine hit of the day.

"Besides Mr Phillips there's two people waiting to see you, Mr Donahue, and here are your messages." She dropped them on his desk and left; she knew how irascible Bill could be. He glanced at them, flicked through his mail, then someone from marketing appeared, asking a question that got lost in the sudden ringing of the phone. His secretary ushered in a customer before he was ready and Bill felt his anger ignite into the dull rage that twisted in his stomach. He took several deep breaths; his working day had begun.

By one o'clock he'd had enough. His eyes felt gritty and the desire to punch someone was almost overwhelming. His in tray was piled high, the phone rang constantly and his computer had just crashed, losing hours of work. He brought angry fists down hard on his desk, knocking a photograph of his wife and daughter to the floor. He snatched it up and stared at them furiously. Both of them smiling smugly into the camera, both spending his hard earned cash, expecting him to bring home more, always wanting, wanting, wanting. His wife seemed to think that their bank account was a never-ending pool to be drained at will; she wanted a conservatory, a holiday in America, a new car. His grip tightened furiously on the plastic photograph frame. And as for his daughter, well he hadn't seen or spoken to her for nearly a year. They'd had a terrible row, although now he couldn't remember what it was about, and she'd packed her bags and left. Mind you he was still paying for her. He knew she called home when he was out and that his wife gave her money, funded her lavish lifestyle. God, when would it ever end? He slammed the photo face down on the desk with unnecessary force.

"Mr Ridley wants to know why you didn't see him yesterday?" his secretary said, breaking into his curdled thoughts. "And Peter in accounts needs those figures right away." She retreated before he exploded.

He closed his eyes, he didn't feel well and for the first time in his working life he decided to leave the office early and go home. He packed his briefcase and walked out, leaving his secretary open mouthed.

Once in his car he sat for a moment, trying to get a grip on his temper, breathing deeply. He couldn't remember when he'd last felt relaxed or happy. He was always rushing, always stretched too tight, always trying to keep up but always slipping behind. He closed his eyes and massaged his aching temples.

"Hey Bill, bad luck about young Roger getting promoted above you." The voice was full of malice. Bill's eyes snapped open to see the smug expression of a colleague pressed up against the car window. "Better luck next time, eh?" And the face retreated, grinning spitefully.

Bill felt like he'd been punched. So he'd been overlooked yet again, had he? Next year he'd be fifty-five, maybe they'd ease him out. Then how would he pay all the bills and his millstone of a mortgage? His headache increased and he was suddenly intolerably hot.

He started his car and gunned it towards the road. He drove in furious spurts exchanging rude hand signals with other drivers as traffic lights; buses and road works slowed his progress. Once out of the city he got stuck behind a caravan and nearly got himself killed in a reckless attempt at overtaking it. His face was mottled with rage as he weaved behind the offending vehicle, hooting his horn and howling futile insults. All rational thought had left his head, his anger consumed him.

Finally, he turned off the easiest route home onto narrower country lanes to lose the caravan. Much lighter traffic allowed him to speed until he came up behind a brand new Vauxhall doing only thirty miles an hour. He was instantly furious at having to slow down and all his resentment focused on the unfortunate driver in front of him. The final straw.

The brake lights blinked as the Vauxhall crept carefully around a bend and Bill's rage threatened to choke him. Bloody Sunday morning driver, out for a cruise in his new car! Bill's lips were pulled back in a snarl and he accelerated until their bumpers kissed briefly. He kept his hand on the horn and waved a fist at the frightened eyes looking back at him in the rear view mirror.

"Get out of the way, you cretin!" he screamed, spit bubbling on his lips. The Vauxhall increased its speed but it wasn't enough for Bill, he remained hard up behind it. He'd finally found someone he could bully. He knew he was frightening the driver in front but it felt good, he needed someone to pay for all the indignities that life was throwing at him.

The Vauxhall accelerated again in an attempt to lose the madness on its tail but Bill was stuck like glue. The car weaved across the white line as terrified eyes looked back in the mirror and not at the road ahead. Then it careered too fast around a sharp bend and the driver lost the battle. Tyres screeched, brake lights flashed and the car hit the grass verge, skidded out of control and flipped onto its back before crashing into the lake that bordered the road.

Bill saw it all happen in slow motion. Saw the tremendous cascade of water explode upwards, the noise, the frenzied hiss and splutter of escaping air. He stopped his car immediately, he knew the driver would be trying to escape but he didn't do anything. He sat numbly watching, all anger gone, staring until the Vauxhall sank below the surface and only part of the tyres remained above the water, the ripples spreading in an ever widening circle. Then silence. Wiping the sweat from his hands he put his car into gear and drove away.

He parked in a lay-by a few miles on where reaction set in and he began to shake. He vomited onto the grass verge and he realised that he was crying. The awfulness of what he'd done descended like a downpour, soaking into every fibre of his body. He'd killed someone. His anger had consumed him and he'd caused an accident, someone had died.

He needed to get home. He needed to ring the police and report a murder.

★ ★ ★

Ironically the drive back to his house took him twice as long as normal. He drove with exaggerated care, kept rigidly to the speed limit and had to stop several times to be sick. As he finally turned into his road he was appalled to see that a police car was already there, parked in his driveway. Someone had obviously reported the crash, must have seen him and taken his number plate as he sped away. He felt ill and deeply ashamed. His wife was talking to two police officers by the front door but she ran to him in tears as soon as he got out of his car. The two policemen followed more slowly and Bill tried to speak, to confess, but the words got stuck in his throat.

One of the policemen reached out and touched his arm. Their expressions were sombre, their eyes unreadable. Bill swallowed, and opened his mouth like a dying fish gasping for air. His wife was holding onto the lapels of his suit and shaking him, her face crumpled in anguish.

"Oh why Bill, why?" Her voice cracked. He covered her hands with his own and tried to answer but she wasn't listening.

"Why?" she gasped again, racked by sobs. "She was only coming home to show me her new car."

He frowned in confusion and looked over her head at the grave faces of the two policemen. A terrible thought was forming, a nightmare in the middle of the afternoon.

"I don't understand," he said, but he had a dreadful feeling that he did.

One of the policemen coughed and cleared his throat. "We're sorry to have to tell you this sir," he said "but your daughter, Alison Donahue has been involved in a fatal accident."

Bill shut his eyes to try and cut off the rest of the terrible words that he knew were coming.

"Her car has been found in a lake next to the B1128. There's a series of very sharp bends," the policeman murmured gently. "She must having been travelling too fast. The car was new, she wouldn't have been used to it. We don't think anyone else was involved."

An Interesting Afternoon
- Melanie Keast -

T he old man had no warning that he was about to pass
out as he cycled along the disused railway track in the
hot midday sunshine. His day suddenly turned black and
his thin body collapsed like a rag doll onto his handlebars,
before he and his bike toppled untidily to the ground.

The three young boys, coming fast from the opposite
direction found him only moments later. They too were on
bikes and filling in a boring summer's afternoon by having
a race from one end of the three-mile track to the other.
Spider, so called because his surname was Mann, was
leading, and as he rounded the bend he was looking back
over his shoulder at his panting mates, working hard to
catch him up.

'You two couldn't catch a cold!' he howled smugly
before glancing forwards again. He saw the bike and the
body too late and with no time to stop took avoiding action
in the knee-high nettles edging the path. The two boys
behind had longer to react and slewed their bikes sideways
like motorcross riders, legs braced, elbows locked, stopping
in a cloud of dust with only inches to spare.

Spider swore loudly as he hopped nimbly out of the stingers, dragging his bike behind him and scratching at his bare legs. 'What's going on?' he demanded angrily of no one in particular.

'It's an old geezer, init?' said Init in surprise, his nickname obvious to anyone who listened to him for more than a few seconds. The third boy, Brian, just shrugged his shoulders, pursing his lips as he stared impassively at the human obstruction.

The old man lay half under his bike in a twisted heap. He was wearing a long raincoat buttoned right up to the neck in spite of the hot day, and one Wellington boot, the other having come off when he'd fallen from the bike. Rather bizarrely, he also was wearing pink washing up gloves and a red spotted handkerchief, tied the way cowboys do with a knot at the back of his neck. His eyes were closed and there was blood on his forehead where he'd connected with the handlebars on his way down.

'He looks dead,' remarked Brian, as if discussing nothing more important than the day's weather.

Spider continued to rub at the stings on his legs but leaned in closer to look at the body. He had no desire to touch a dead person but as the self elected boss of his small gang this was a chance to show how brave he was and flex his leadership muscle.

'He's probably been murdered,' whispered Init fearfully. 'Bludgeoned to death with a hammer an' been lying here crying for help for ages, and now we've arrived just a bit too late.'

Brian sneered. 'You're daft, you are. How's he going to call for help if he's been murdered? He'd be dead wouldn't he an' the dead can't talk!' And he punched Init playfully on the arm who then retaliated with a swift kick at his shins.

Spider shushed them and motioned for Brian to lift the man's bicycle away before moving nearer to the comatose old bloke. He had a lot of clothes on for such a hot day and what was with the rubber gloves? Maybe he'd got something horribly contagious on his hands or better still maybe he hadn't got any hands at all, just mechanical fingers like a robot. Spider reluctantly put a brake on his fertile imagination and pressed his hand to the wrinkled neck.

'Hey, you can't strangle him!' Init sounded aghast.

Brian sniggered. 'He's just feeling for a pulse, dummy. You know, to see if he's dead or not. You must've seen it on the telly, they always do that when there's been an accident.'

Init looked interested and moved a little closer. 'Is he?' he asked hopefully. He'd never seen a dead body before and one wearing pink washing up gloves would be a bonus. Spider shrugged, he didn't know, the man felt warm but he couldn't find a pulse. Mind you, he wasn't at all sure that he was feeling in the right place.

'Shouldn't you loosen his clothing or something?' suggested Brian, swatting lazily at a passing butterfly. 'They do that on the telly too.'

'I was just going to,' Spider retorted, annoyed at not having thought of it first. He knelt down next to the old man and undid his raincoat to reveal a grey v - necked jumper with a fleecy checked shirt underneath. Christ, the old bloke had probably cooked himself wearing this lot, no wonder he'd come off his bike. He glanced up at the cloudless blue sky and the sun shining mercilessly down on them before undoing the top two buttons of the shirt to expose the old geezer's wrinkled throat. Then he lifted each limp arm and carefully peeled off the rubber gloves, revealing gnarled hands but disappointingly no suppurating sores or metal fingers, before sitting back on his heels to survey his handiwork.

Init let out a suppressed breath and the three of them relaxed as they considered what to do next.

Spider had an idea first and pressed his ear onto the old man's chest to see if he could hear his heart beating.

'Christ! What're you doing?' Init sounded amazed. 'Giving him a hug ain't going to help!'

Brian snorted with laughter and Init bridled. 'Well it's daft, init?' he whined, aware that he'd said something stupid but not sure what. He was nine, two years younger than the other two and not the sharpest card in the pack.

'Ssshhhhh!' Spider hissed, his head still pressed to the narrow chest. He listened intently for several moments before sitting up. 'He's alive,' he proclaimed with all the authority of a doctor and Brian grunted without much interest.

'He probably fainted in this heat.' Spider glanced again at the sun. 'Give us a hand Bri, let's get his coat off. Fan him with something, Init. If we cool him down he'll probably come round.'

Init, always eager to please, picked up the nearest thing to him, which happened to be the Wellington boot that had come off the old man when he'd collapsed. Not the easiest of objects to waft around, but what Init lacked in style he made up for in enthusiasm. On his third swing a twenty-pound note fluttered gently onto the prone body and before Init could stop waving the wellie, a further bundle of twenties had followed.

No one spoke.

Then Spider let out a low whoop, Brian's bored expression vanished and Init stuck his hand inside the boot and withdrew one last note. The boys stared at each other in amazed silence, then Init snatched off the other Wellington that the old man still had on and shook it vigorously. Nothing. Init peered inside and shook his head.

'It's empty, init?' he said with disappointment. 'Must've made him walk a bit funny though.'

Brian giggled but Spider was looking at the big pile of money with awe. He glanced quickly up and down the track but it was completely deserted so he grabbed the old man's raincoat and felt in one of the pockets.

'Jeez!' he exclaimed as he withdrew a thick bundle of ten-pound notes. Brian gasped and excitedly thrust his hand into the other pocket and pulled out some more.

'That's a lotta money, init?' said Init. 'Who is this bloke?'

Spider shook his head and the three boys grinned at each other. This was turning out to be one interesting afternoon.

'Look in his trouser pockets,' Init suggested, with a flash of rare intuition. 'He might have something with his name on.'

Spider wiped his nose on the back of his hand and glanced up in surprise. 'Good idea,' he said grudgingly and Init turned pink with pleasure. But all the old man had in his pockets was more money, this time, fifties in two neatly bound packs, with the amount printed on each bundle. Everyone was lost for words until Spider suddenly remembered that as the leader he should be making the decisions and stood up importantly.

'Right, Init, you cycle to the village and get some help. This stupid ol' bloke's lucky it's us that's found him. Anyone else would've nicked the cash and left him to die.' Init hesitated, loath to leave such an exciting discovery plus all that money. 'Go on, bring the law back or someone who'll know what to do,' urged Spider. 'We might get a reward for helping him. He's got more than enough.'

Init dawdled about for a few more moments before the two older boys watched him reluctantly pick up his bike and cycle away, raising a small cloud of dust as he pedalled furiously up the still deserted track. Brian began fanning the old man's face with a wad of twenties while Spider gathered the rest of the money together in one large pile next to him. He was just about to stuff it all back into the raincoat pockets when the old man's eyes snapped open and stared accusingly at him. Brian stopped fanning and Spider fell back in shock. A bony hand shot out and fastened itself around Spider's wrist and the old man abruptly sat up.

'Little buggers,' he snarled, his lips drawn back to reveal ill-fitting false teeth. 'Pinch my money, would yer?' His eyes looked like shiny black beads and his grip was surprisingly strong.

'No mister,' said Spider, alarmed. 'I was going....'

'Yeah, I know you was going,' the man shouted, spraying Spider with spittle. 'You was going off with my money! You don't know who you're messing with boy!' He snatched a wad of notes from Spider's hand and climbed to his feet. 'I'm Ronnie Biggs!'

The two boys sniggered in spite of their growing nervousness; the old git was obviously nuts. They knew Ronnie Biggs was dead because it'd been in the papers so this old fart certainly wasn't him.

'Think that's funny, do yer?' the old man roared and unbelievably, on that ordinary, hot afternoon in August he pulled a gun from the waistband of his trousers. He pointed it at them and they froze, their eyes wide with disbelief and real fear.

'I'm the great train robber, Ronnie Biggs,' the old man crowed feverishly. 'Only I don't bother with trains no more.' He looked down and with his free hand began stuffing the money carefully back into his raincoat pockets. The two boys started inching backwards towards their bikes but the old man stopped them with a wave of his gun, the sun glancing off the polished barrel.

'Don't move!' he warned and the boys stopped immediately, sweat beading their top lips. 'Scared?' he sneered. 'Well you should be cos I just might have to kill you now you've seen my face!'

Spider and Brian stood shoulder to shoulder and shook their heads furiously.

'We'd never recognise you again, mister, honest. I don't remember nothing, do you, Bri?'

'Nothing,' Brian agreed, wondering if he'd have time to get away if the mad old git shot Spider first.

The old man didn't look convinced but he was more interested in collecting up the cash, which, with only one hand was taking him longer than he'd have liked. He was also finding it very tiring in the unrelenting heat of the afternoon so he sat down again, motioning with the gun for the boys to do the same. 'Sit,' he commanded, waggling the gun barrel. 'Sit down.' He seemed to find this very funny and started to laugh, which quickly turned to a chesty wheeze followed by a coughing fit, during which his false teeth were shaken loose. His eyes closed momentarily but when their wrinkled lids lifted again his glare was every bit as menacing as before. He pushed his teeth back into place and said proudly, 'I've just done a robbery.'

'No kidding,' scoffed Brian, 'and here's us thinking you was just rich.' But his irony seemed lost on the old man who was back to gathering his money. 'Yep, forced 'em to open the safe and took the lot. Every last bundle of money.' He looked casually at Brian. 'They didn't think I was joking. They was really scared, the women screamed and everything! I had to shoot them of course, to shut them up,' and then he smiled and carefully aimed the gun at the sweat that was running down between Brian's eyebrows.

Spider swallowed, his throat very dry as his friend sagged in fear against his shoulder. He was too frightened to move or think and it was with immense relief that he suddenly heard distant raised voices and the faint thud of running feet coming their way. The old bloke's eyes widened and he turned round to look up the track.

'You've told the coppers!' he snarled, his black eyes glittering angrily as he climbed to his feet and he pointed the gun at them with renewed enthusiasm. But then, just like in all the best movies, the cavalry came into view, charging around the bend, raising dust and coming to their aid.

Init, on his bicycle, was leading the way with a policeman and two paramedics carrying a stretcher, trotting smartly behind him. Further back was a nurse in a blue uniform; all were very red in the face and out of breath.

The old man spat furiously on the ground, thrust the gun back into his waistband and began struggling into his raincoat. He made no attempt to run away and instead spent valuable time gathering up the remaining bundles of money and trying to pull on his Wellington boots. The posse arrived just as he finished and he was surrounded.

Spider and Brian stood up, still holding on to each other.

'Mr Fanshaw,' began the policeman, between gasps but the old man just looked mutinous. The nurse stepped forward and touched the policeman's shoulder. 'Let me,' she whispered. 'He thinks he's the great train robber.' She turned to him with an encouraging smile. 'Come on now Mr Biggs, it's time for you to come back with me. You really did frighten everyone in the office you know. They were very impressed at the way you held them up, but you've got to give them back the money.'

The old man looked sulky and folded his arms across his narrow chest like a chastised child.

'He's got a gun,' hissed Spider hoarsely but the nurse smiled and shook her head. 'No dear, it's not real.' And she reached over and took it out of his waistband. 'It's only a toy.'

Looking at it now, in the safety of being with everybody else, it was perfectly obvious that it was a cheap imitation but to cover their embarrassment Spider said hotly; 'Well we knew that, didn't we Brian? We were just trying to keep the nutter here until you all arrived.'

'I told them,' piped Init, anxious to remind them of his part in it all. 'That's right, init?' he said to the policeman, who nodded his agreement. 'The old git robbed the safe in the office, that's where all this money came from and why he wore those gloves. Finger prints.' Init tapped the side of his nose and nodded knowingly, his face flushed with excitement. 'He 'scaped from the nursing home in town this morning. She works there,' he pointed at the nurse, 'an' she says he's bonkers. Thinks he's someone else. Ronnie Corbett, init?' He frowned uncertainly at the policeman who tried not to smile.

'Biggs,' he corrected. 'Ronnie Biggs.'

The policeman waited patiently as the old man was cajoled by the nurse into putting all the stolen money into a bag and handing over it over to him for safekeeping. Then, stubbornly refusing to get on the stretcher, he was led slowly away, before the policeman turned back to the three boys with a smile. 'Well done lads,' he said. 'You all did an excellent job. Call at the station later, there might be a small reward for being so honest. I expect the nursing home will be pleased to get their patient and their money back so quickly.'

Spider, Brian and Init watched the strange little group walk away. The old git, supported by the two paramedics, the nurse following with his bike and the policeman bringing up the rear with a bag of money.

'An interesting afternoon,' mused Spider. 'D'you think anyone will believe us when we tell them we met Ronnie Biggs in pink rubber gloves after he'd robbed the nursing home with a toy gun?' They all howled with laughter and punched each other playfully before climbing on their bikes.

'Doubt it,' grunted Init, putting his hand in his pocket and rubbing his grimy fingers over one of the twenty-pound notes he'd palmed. 'But it is true, init?'

Graham Penn

Graham Penn is a retired police officer who was presented with his long service and good conduct medal by Prince Charles in 1996. He now works as an art technician in a local High School. Having run the London marathon twice he now restricts himself to walking and cycling in the North Norfolk countryside where he lives with his wife June. His other interests are swimming, tennis, cooking and photography.

Graham is presently working on a crime story and drawing on his past experience as a Norwich Police Officer.

Graham Penn

The Cycle Of Life
- Graham Penn -

"ALL IS WELL WITH THE WORLD"
Adamski Fifteen awoke to read these words on his visual alarm. Yes, he thought, all is well with the world and particularly today and with my world. Today was the day he and Evelyn Sixteen were to embark on the adventure of their life. They were to be the first humans to leave their community since the Reformation. In fact the first humans to leave any community since that world saving period.

He woke refreshed both from the sleep and the sustenance that he had absorbed over the last eight hours. He removed the sustenance tube from his arm and dressed for exercise. He left his home pod and made his way to the gym and joined his companions for a hard, invigorating work out.

He was feeling a little different today and knew that he was excited but emotion was discouraged, how do you prevent it though. He ran hard, cycled furiously but could not rid himself of this feeling. Better keep it to himself, it would be a shame to be replaced at the crucial moment.

Time to be briefed.

"ALL IS WELL WITH THE WORLD"

Evelyn Sixteen woke to the alarm and read the usual greeting. Yes, she thought, all is well with the world but today I am going to leave it behind. Adamski Fifteen and I are going to do what no one has ever done. Evelyn removed the sustenance tube and dressed for exercise, this morning she chose to use the pool. She worked hard and emerged exhilarated.

She returned to her pod and sat at the computer reading her latest messages. Why did she feel so strange? The word fear sprang to mind but emotions were no longer part of the human make up. Life was good, she knew that, and she was at her prime in her third decade. So why did she feel so odd, you can't ask the computer that sort of question can you?

Anyway, time to go to briefing, keep it to yourself, any sign of emotion and they might decide to replace her which would be a shame after only three decades.

"ALL IS WELL WITH THE WORLD"

Petrov Twenty woke to the usual irritating message and yanked out the sustenance tube before getting dressed for his exercise time. He put on his walking clothes and went to the walkway. He spent half an hour strutting up and down. His mind firmly set on the day ahead. This was the greatest moment of his era, all eight decades of it, yet he felt out of sorts. He knew what it was. He was grumpy but why? Humans don't have feelings any more, we simply exist for the good of the community. Crap!

He had been feeling this way sometime but had done all he could to hide it from the others as his – no the community's task- would not be finalised without him. He knew that his time was up and whilst he understood the principal of move on and let others carry on, he still thought he had another decade in him!

Anyway, time for the briefing.

★ ★ ★

"THE WORLD IS A MESS"
It all came to a head at the beginning of the 21st. Century. It became the common belief that humanity was destroying the world through its excesses. Environmental issues were cool especially to politicians who had lost popularity, celebrities who had nothing else to spend their fortunes on, lawyers who wanted someone else to sue and a media who had nothing interesting to write about.

The truth of the matter was that the world was warming just as it had been since the ice age! That was why the ice melted – duh!

It was also true that the humans were not helping matters but they were not in danger of destroying the world. What they were doing was destroying an environment that sustained their life. The world would happily continue for a few million years yet, with or without the human race.

It was the arrogance of man that would be his undoing along with a little greed.

★ ★ ★

Adamski Fifteen, Evelyn Sixteen and Petrov Twenty were all members of community Two Hundred and Thirty Seven and this particular community had one task to address at the moment. The task that the main frame had allocated community Two Hundred and Thirty Seven was to:

"Investigate the plausibility that man evolved from the ape."

It was commonly thought that if the main frame had asked for an investigation that there must be some doubt in the possibility of such a thing.

Now Petrov Twenty had emerged eight decades ago and had applied every known technique and mind available to him and he was loath to leave without an answer even though he knew his follower would continue.

After three decades of unsuccessful work he had the brilliant idea of going to have a look. He developed and perfected the theory of time travel. He had then requested that he be provided with two scientists who were suitable for the field study. Adamski Fifteen and Evelyn Sixteen emerged as his perfect investigators.

The time machine worked on the principal that if a vessel travelled at the speed of light and an individual walked the length of the vessel then they would travel faster than light. These criteria meant there would be a shift in time.

Petrov Twenty perfected this by creating a large vessel that travelled at the speed of light and inserting a smaller vessel that travelled extremely slowly along a helix within the large vessel; it was this smaller vessel that moved through time.

Today would prove him correct.

Adamski Fifteen had emerged three decades ago in order to study the evolution of life on earth and from the start had known that one day he was to travel back in time and observe the beginning of man. To this end he had taken input from every available source and was knowledgeable about every known form of life that had ever existed.

He had particularly concentrated on apes, as he knew that Evelyn Sixteen had emerged in order to study the history of man. They had purposely not spoken of their studies so as not to influence any subsequent observations.

The most enjoyable side of his task had been watching life on earth, as it existed today. This was possible through the use of the satellites that orbited the earth.

Every inch of the world was accessible for viewing. Since The Reformation man had had no influence on the flora, fauna or climate of planet earth but was able to watch every little change. In the 19th century they had perceived the concept of Stewardship. Adamski Fifteen liked to think of himself as a Steward of Nature.

Adamski Fifteen was a product of his time and it troubled him not that he was a small cog in a large wheel. He had all that he needed to enjoy life and knew that it was the contribution of every individual that kept the earth and the human race continuing.

He had read all the books on communism, religion, big brother, freedom of the individual, human rights, fascism, love and just about any other subject you wished to mention. Man had become too full of himself and had lost sight of his insignificance within the universe. It was humility that made the true human.

Prior to The Reformation man had made life so complicated that he was destroying the essence of human good. Now all that existed was the goodness of man in the most simple of forms. It was not complicated by greed, ambition or false emotions.

Evelyn Sixteen specialised in the development of man and unlike Adamski Fifteen did not have the luxury of observing man in his natural state prior to Reformation.

She knew though that the man of today was a product of technology. This fact made modern man extremely dull to study when compared to men of the past.

She did, however, love her work and prided herself on knowing more of man's ancestors and development than any other of her colleagues. She was the scientist best suited to the trip.

The down side to her studies was the realisation of what man had been capable of, the thought of killing was beyond modern man as was the thought of inflicting pain or anguish on another being. In this she was glad of the modern style.

An area of confusion though had arisen when amongst the stories of horror and anguish; there were episodes of physical and emotional love and acts of unselfish bravery. Evelyn Sixteen wondered about these feelings and often pondered whether evil and good existed hand in hand.

Evelyn knew that since The Reformation man had placed himself in the perfect position to oversee the continuance of life on earth. She was glad to be a small part of this and had enjoyed her studies of history.

★ ★ ★

It all started to change in the 2020's when a small country called Iceland made a scientist Prime Minister. This was a first - not only was he a practical man but he was honest!

Up until this date the politicians across the globe had been paying lip service to the environmentalists. The answer to global warming was to legislate and tax and if that failed then legislate and tax some more. It was no good taxing the affluent because they just paid and carried on. It is no good taxing and then not ploughing the money into ameliorating the affects of pollution.

It wasn't rocket science. In order to stop humans from adding to global warming all you had to do was stop producing gases that caused it. No travelling, energy from renewable sources only, reduction of consumption across the board. Probably most controversial of all was a drastic reduction in population.

Iceland, however, did start to completely turn their lifestyle around. It did not happen overnight but it happened reasonably quickly and scientists who had no financial or political agenda oversaw it all. They merely wanted to make the world a cleaner and greener place. Being a small country it was also easy to carry the population along with the innovative way of life.

The number of vehicles halved. 75% of energy was provided through wind, wave motion and thermal tapping. Families were educated in making everything they used last. Throwaway society was recognised for what it really was – wasteful.

Couples were encouraged to have no more than two children but to lavish them with love and care, not money and over education.

The population of Iceland soon noticed that life became easier, less complicated. Money seemed to go further not only due to less wanton spending but also through a lower tax burden. With a happier population, social problems eased and family life strengthened.

By the 2200's Iceland was the leader in environmental issues and was being heralded as the example of the way forward.

The western world had shifted towards a scientific remedy led by scientists.

Governments had set up World Institutes for Scientific Excellence (WISE). Politicians still liked their acronyms!!

Funding was virtually unlimited and the directors of each Institute were left very much to their own devices.

On the face of it the world was becoming a better place to live and green technology was the only acceptable way forward. The world still continued to warm but at a rate that was less due to human influence. The Governments were pleased with themselves and their people were pleased with their Governments.

Meanwhile the directors of the institutes worked hard at their true purpose.

This was to save the human race whilst allowing the world to exist without human influence.

No matter how green humans became there would soon be a day when the earth's environment would be unable to sustain them.

By the end of the 29th Century the earth would have no ozone layer resulting in lethal quantities of ultraviolet light in the sun's rays. Furthermore the earth would be ninety percent covered by water.

The scientists knew that eventually the water would again freeze and the ozone layer reappear. Life, nature, call it what you will, was cyclic and you were never going to change it. The answer was to anticipate and adapt.

In order to adapt you had to reduce the population of seven billion to five million. It was also important that the five million were the right ones to carry on the human gene.

★ ★ ★

Petrov Twenty arrived at the launch room confident that all that could have been done had been, he had covered every aspect of the experiment. Now all that was left for him to do was hand the briefing sheet to the task Director.

Evelyn Fifteen and Adamski Sixteen were in the briefing room, waiting. Petrov Twenty had had little contact with them. This was intentional in order that the each party maintained a professional view of their part. The interaction between different team members could often lead to unnecessary complications. Petrov Twenty had originally asked for only one investigator to be sent. This had been refused on health and safety grounds and for the obvious reason that two minds were greater than one.

Petrov Twenty remained aloof as he wished the two adventurers good luck and handed the briefing sheets to the director. Petrov Twenty left them to be briefed and to board the craft. He went to the control pod, joining the technicians who were responsible for constructing the complicated craft.

Adamski Fifteen and Evelyn Sixteen were already in the briefing room when the director entered. The briefing took little time and the director congratulated them on their hard work and wished them well assuring them that every minor detail had been taken care of.

They entered the craft and secured themselves prior to take off.

Adamski Fifteen looked over to Evelyn Sixteen and said: 'Well here goes, all set.'

'Yes, I'm glad to be getting on with it after all this time. What about you?'

'It has been a while and I can't believe we are finally off. I know it isn't supposed to happen but I am tingling with excitement!'

'Thank goodness for that. I'm worried sick that something might go wrong.'

They both laughed and relaxed which was just as well as the countdown started.

Ten, nine, eight, seven, six, five, for, three, two, one...

★ ★ ★

By the year 2790 WISE had established 1,000 centres/communities each with a selection of scientists, technicians, and computer experts. All of the centres were linked to a mainframe computer which was linked to a number of satellites.

The world politicians, whilst eagerly financing WISE and reaping the positive spin of a green world, had failed to notice a number of things. Each centre was a self sufficient Biosphere and they were all located above 2,000 metres!

The world at large had no idea how WISE operated and if the politicians had been a little more astute they would have become suspicious of the fact that WISE no longer needed financing.

Each community had a population of 5,000 people within which there were no politicians, lawyers or financiers. Every member had a purpose specific to the running of the community and the subsequent Stewardship of Earth.

Each community was populated by individuals whose physical, social and intellectual needs were entirely fulfilled within and by the community. This precluded the need for currency. No money – no lawyers!

Individuals were cloned and emerged as adults and had annual health checks.

Towards the end of their time they would not return from a health check and a clone would emerge. There was no fear of death as your clone was yourself. There was the added bonus of a society without teenagers!

Molecular configuration enabled all organic and inorganic substance to be created. The communities were able to create any substance that they wished. All needs could be provided for from within the community. There was no need to farm, hunt, mine, travel or inter react at all outside of the community. The interference level with the earth was nil.

The Biospheres were the size of a small town and were built down into the earth so as to be insulated by earth. The domes were built of a material that was unbreakable, clear and filtered out the harmful UV. Energy was gained from three sources. Thermal energy from deep below the earth's crust. Wind energy from turbines dotted around the biospheres' periphery. The currents of the sea had also been harnessed by anchoring giant turbines at strategic positions deep in the ocean. These huge waterwheels turned as the prevailing current passed through them. Each biosphere was linked to all of three different energy sources and could exist exclusively on any one of these methods.

Each biosphere was equipped with an argonium reactor that allowed nuclear fusion and clean energy. The resultant waste from fusion was the inert gas argon. Argonium had been discovered in the earth's mantle and only a small amount resulted in a massive amount of energy. It was this substance that was used to power the time craft.

With everything in place and all of the biospheres interlinked to each other and now completely independent of the rest of the world it was time for lockdown. This involved cutting all ties with the outer populace. All of the computer systems outside of the biospheres were turned off.

By this time humans were completely dependent on computer technology and WISE had even encouraged further dependence knowing that one day it would make things easier when the time came to go it alone.

This period was known as The Reformation and it came at a time when the world's ecosystem was becoming human unfriendly. The seas had risen covering the majority of the land and the sun's rays were now totally unfiltered of UV rays.

The outer population was about to perish.

★ ★ ★

Petrov Twenty, the director and the technicians all watched as the craft disappeared and a small cheer of success went up.

Petrov Twenty, however, looked concerned and said, 'Oh dear!'

The director looked a little confused. 'What do you mean, "Oh dear."? All has gone as planned. Hasn't it?'

' No, not really. The craft hasn't returned.'

The Director was not a patient man at the best of times and snapped, 'Don't be so silly. They are scheduled to be investigating for sixty days.'

'Quite so, but once they had completed the investigation the craft was to return to our time thirty seconds after leaving. That would save a lot of hanging about on our part.'

'So the automatic return sequence was set for now.'

'Yes but it isn't automatic as they have to set the start program. It was carefully detailed in the briefing sheet."

Now the director was visibly shaking - not a good sign! 'There was nothing in the briefing sheet about the return sequence. We all presumed it was automatic.'

Petrov Twenty thought that to presume was a mistake but held his tongue. 'The last page of the briefing sheet had the full instructions on the return process.'

As he said this he noticed that on his less than tidy desk sat the last page of the briefing pack. He cursed the working group who had decided that staplers were an unacceptable health and safety risk.

The director asked the obvious question, 'How do we get them back?'

'We can't. They will sit waiting for the automatic return and then think it has failed. They are not trained to program the return themselves. Silly thing is they only have to push one button but it is carefully hidden away to prevent accidental operation. This was all carefully laid out in the briefing sheet.'

'That will be the briefing sheet you never gave to me! What are the risks of environmental interference with them staying on earth out of their time? Will there be a butterfly effect?'

Petrov Twenty quickly grasped the point and was pleased that he had thought through this eventuality. He activated the world monitors that gave updates on the current status of each biosphere and then the monitors that attended to the outside status. All was well with the world.

He said, 'It would seem that there has been no adverse effect as there has been no changes and we are all here. The craft and all it contained are biodegradable and should break down rapidly. The scientists will be unable to survive long without their craft.'

The Director considered the situation and though pleased that there was no long term damage he was disappointed that the years of work had come to nothing with no way of recovering the situation. He looked at Petrov Twenty and said, 'Do you think that it may be time for your medical check?'

Petrov Twenty was in no position to argue as he had lasted longer than most and had certainly enjoyed the task given to him. He knew that life would continue in the form of Petrov Twenty One. So off he trudged.

★ ★ ★

The lockout was well co-ordinated and the 1,000 biospheres were well prepared as was the five million population within them.

The outside population were not at all prepared and pandemonium ensued. Every single system that the human race had come to depend on was connected to a computer. The mainframe was controlled by the insiders and with lockout all outside, terminals went down. Transport, health and hygiene, communications, finance, military, record keeping, every single aspect of human life was thrown into confusion.

The population was much smaller than it had been in the twentieth century and now stood at about 850 million people. Politicians declared a state of emergency and called upon the emergency services to act immediately, however planning contingencies were lost as was the ability to communicate.

The remaining population soon realised that food and water would soon become scarce. Ordinary people were forced to steal from shops and hoard what they could for the future. To prevent this the army and police were ordered to patrol the streets and shoot offenders on sight. Anarchy soon took over and people were killing each other.

Starvation, thirst and disease started to take its toll. The food and water systems had been run by computers, as had the hospitals, so there was no relief for the suffering population.

The armed services were tasked with trying to gain access to the biospheres in order to secure the mainframe and coerce the inside population into restoring the systems. The biospheres had been built in the most remote of locations and of course without computers airplanes and ships were useless. The few missile systems left in the world were also inoperable.

Soldiers did manage to reach a few of the biospheres but with their meagre hand weapons an assault was useless.

Small pockets of the outside population did manage to exist for a little time but with little food and water, no medicines and an increasingly hostile environment particularly from the sun's rays and encroaching sea, these were all gone 200 years after lockout.

★ ★ ★

Petrov Twenty walked the short distance to the medical centre as slowly as he could, not through fear, but through a nagging doubt that he had missed something.

The failure of the craft to return with no subsequent effect on the present world may just have been luck. Or it may have a more significant meaning. Was it possible that the craft's arrival in the past was part of the future?

Petrov Twenty was racking his brain for a small piece he had studied many years ago that had involved a rather absurd book called the Bible. He recalled how it had meant so much to many and how millions had perished fighting over their differing beliefs fuelled by this one book whose author was pretty much unknown. He recalled that the book had been ridiculed by the scientific community and had not been part of The Reformation.

How did this have anything to do with his lifelong task should he return and mention it to the director? It could do no harm and he turned to go back...

It was at this point that the sun imploded and all life ceased.

The End

★ ★ ★

The journey was over as soon as it had started and the control panel indicated that it was safe for the two explorers to leave the craft.

Adamski Fifteen and Evelyn Sixteen emerged from the craft and were struck silent. They were overcome by a tsunami of sensation.

There were so many colours of such deep and bright hues that were beyond anything that they had previously seen or ever imagined. Noises that changed every second and were beyond recognition. Their noses were assailed by aromas that were sometimes pleasant and sometimes not so pleasant but all so new. Their skin was experiencing warmth directly from the sun and a breeze that cooled them at the same time.

None of this was under anyone's control and in that lay the excitement.

They did not speak for fifteen minutes and they turned to each other, both already smiling and with tears in their eyes.

Evelyn Sixteen said, 'I know what it means to be born now.'

Adamski Fifteen took her hand and said, 'Let's explore.'

They were in the plains of central Africa some one hundred thousand years ago when, according to dubious historical theories, Homo Sapiens was in its ascendancy and starting to migrate north. It was a beautiful lush landscape and it was difficult for them to take in all that they experienced. The briefing and their expectations had not prepared them for the enormity of their adventure. They both felt at one with nature. Equally the wildlife that they experienced took little notice of them. There was neither fear nor threat on either part.

They returned to the craft and sat outside as the sun dipped in the sky, bringing on a wealth of new colours. They were both flushed with excitement.

Adam said, 'This may sound silly but for the first time in my life I actually feel alive.'

She quietly replied, 'Not silly at all but very true and we have got six weeks to enjoy it.'

He turned and looked at her. 'Or the rest of our lives.'

'Would you be happy to stay here?'

'Would you?'

She thought for a full minute. 'Yes I could live with this.'

'And me.'

'Oh yes and you, but please call me Eve and not Evelyn Sixteen.'

' I'll settle for a simple Adam.'

They both pondered the future for a while and then Adam had a thought. 'We may need some help if we are going to settle here and I can't see any evidence of early man at all.'

'No but we haven't got the equipment to start cloning more of us.'

He grinned at her, saying, ' I think that we have.'

She smiled coyly and said,' Well no time like the present.' She got up and walked into the craft and, looking over her shoulder, she called out, ' Come on then.'

Graham Penn

Stella Robbins

Stella Robbins has lived a quiet almost contemplative life in Belfast, London, Newcastle Co. Down and some other places as well. Until she joined Kelvin I. Jones' writing class in Norfolk she had attempted nothing in the way of creative writing and nobody had ever evinced the least interest in anything she had to say. No matter how loudly she said it. In this field, therefore, as well as in several others, the glare of fame's spotlight has never, till now, fallen upon her. She feels confident, however, that she will not be dazzled by it.

Stella Robbins

Her Ladyship's Address
- Stella Robbins -

To begin with, let me say how delighted I am to be here to talk to you all this evening. I remember this beautiful hall from the days when I used to attend the performances of his own heaven born music which were given here by Mr. Handel. At the present time, of course, the inconvenience to myself of appearing in public in this way is obviously considerable, since the risk of attack is so great that very tight security now surrounds my every move. But I make a point of honouring my engagements, no matter what kind of commotion is going on. Really, sometimes one gets the impression that the world is full of ruffians.

Naturally you all know who I am but, for etiquette's sake, allow me to introduce myself. I am recognized always as Lady London, formerly Londinium of the mighty Roman empire and today a vast and vital city and the great financial capital of the world, but my heritage has always been most enviably illustrious and distinguished and its influence extended to all the corners of the globe. I mention this, my dear people, not because I am unduly self-laudatory but because there are times, such as the present, when self-effacement is patently ridiculous. That being understood, I need have no hesitation in acknowledging that I have received more accolades and acclaim in my lifetime than I could easily relate but perhaps, if I were to choose the merely personal tribute which pleased me most, it would be the one paid me around the time of my eighteenth century when that dear old windbag, Dr. Johnson, took it into his head to write some choleric verse about the riffraff who would damage my name and then gallantly declared that a man who was tired of London (between ourselves he always used to call me his Intoxicating Temptress) was tired of life. Of course, the good Doctor had, I suspect, rather an eye for the ladies but, even were this not the case, it is widely recognized that my own feminine allurements have always been very remarkable, and indeed are still considered so to this day. Though it's best nowadays to be extremely careful how you compliment or describe anything or, before you know where you are, you're likely to find yourself accused of being an 'Ism' or an 'Ist', or some such thing, and quite possibly arrested and charged into the bargain. So very tiresome.

However we needn't concern ourselves too much with the antics and absurdities of the present moment, especially since, as I have often observed before now, current mores, like current fashion, can be as much a question of control as of expression, and every bit as likely to have been tailored to suit someone else's purposes, rather than your own. I myself have seen many styles come and go in the course of my two thousand years and experience has taught me that it's best to maintain a dignified composure in the face of the ludicrous posturings of humankind and the unveiling of some of its more outrageous designs. Indeed, during various periods of my life, I have had to preserve a quite remarkable sangfroid (a modicum of French seeped into my structure during the Norman Conquest) and this coolness I have kept under circumstances of such vexation and harassment as would startle the calm of the most po faced Stoic and try the patience of the most phlegmatic saint. But, as I always say, I will not be provoked.

And here, I hope that I am not going to disappoint a little, for I see that you are all on the edges of your seats, agog with the expectation that I am about to disclose every fascinating detail of my own extraordinary life. But sadly, my dear creatures, the time allowed us this evening is so short that I am compelled to select only a small part of the whole and concentrate on that alone. It would have given me such delight to lead you, as the winding Thames, through my rich and turbulent history (of which I could give a very different account than that provided by some historians). Or to hold you spellbound by the descriptions of all my famously beautiful buildings (tactfully overlooking those structures that are proof of the unfortunate mental peculiarities to which architects and planners, poor lambs, are so often prone). However, these peculiarities can certainly be said to provide something for everyone – especially the property developers – and those of you now inclined to take violent exception to the sublimity that gleams in the dome of St. Paul's, have the glittering summit of the Gherkin on which to feast your eyes.

Of course, you may have come to this talk hoping that I would spirit you away from my solid structures to the aerial magic of literary London. And, though naturally I must be careful to betray no confidences, I can so far indulge you in this as to say that, besides the dear old Doctor, I do remember some of my earliest literary friends with particular fondness. Dearest Chaucer, or Geoffo, as I generally called him, and my amorous Pepys were, at different times, the most delightful company possible and, I'm thankful to say, always had the courtesy to tone down their language a little when they were with me, and most certainly would not have indulged in any bawdiness of behaviour in my presence, for it's well known that I never could abide it. And as to darling Dickens, although our opinions did not always coincide – I was never able to share his enthusiasm for the paintings of Hogarth, for instance – still, on the whole, we got on together famously, and even collaborated, as I'm sure you are all aware, to form a period known as Dickensian London, hoping by this to draw attention to the plight of the desperate souls living in conditions almost too terrible to bear. Often, indeed, do the troubles of those dear beings who are in my care weigh upon me with a great burden of heaviness, and then I find myself turning to the perennial sunshine of 'Plum' (perhaps more readily recognized amongst you as P.G. Wodehouse) to help me see that nothing is of weightier matter than lightness of heart. In more recent times, the writer and scholar Kelvin I. Jones (I am not sufficiently well acquainted with the gentleman to be more informal) has taught me, with the utmost skill and patience, that even I, unlikely though it may seem, continue to need the benefit of knowledge and experience other that my own.

But enthralling though all these things must undoubtedly be to you, the time allowed us now is so brief that we can linger over none of them. What I propose instead is to tell you a little story regarding a part of my greatness that is often overlooked, though almost as essential to us all as air itself. I allude, of course, to my wonderful gardens, sometimes referred to (rather indelicately, I consider) as the Lungs of London. Whether this anatomical description is meant as a reference to the verdant loveliness of my public parks, or to the more modest claims of my ordinary little private gardens, I am not prepared to say and, in any case, it is largely irrelevant, for we all love a garden, no matter what form it takes. Indeed there are those who maintain that the whole baffling predicament of life first began in a garden. Be that as it may, I can't help feeling that a garden in London is an especial treat. And I recollect, one drowsy summer's afternoon a couple of centuries ago, when the song of birds and the hum of bees was in the air and the sweet scent of honeysuckle was all around us, that I happened to be discussing the question with that good, gentle soul, Charles Lamb and he turned to me, making a quizzical little bow and said, with barely a hint of his stammer, 'A garden's a garden anywhere, ma'am, but twice a garden in London.'

Well, it is of two ordinary unsung London gardens that I want now to tell you, and of the friction that arose between them, or rather between their owners, the trouble being caused, as it usually is, by a collision of interests; in this case by what was then seen as The New seeming to challenge and threaten all the beloved safe certainties of The Old, causing so much alarm and perturbation, in consequence, that what started as merely frontier incidents and skirmishes looked likely to develop into pitched and bloody battle. If, therefore, you care to hear the story, you must prepare yourselves for a short journey, for we have to travel together through time some forty three odd years or so.

Be so good then as to settle yourselves comfortably in your seats and return with me, if you will, to the 1960s, a decade regarded by historians as one of seismic change and importance in London and, by inference, the world; and a time when the hydrogen bomb and the space race became part of the mass imagination. To me, of course, there was nothing new or startling to be observed. I had seen it all before in one form or another. Nevertheless, I remember being mildly amused by the various ways the human animal chose to manifest its perceived new freedoms and discoveries at that particular time. Vidal Sassoon haircuts, Mary Quant clothes, Biba Boutiques, Carnaby Street, Beatlemania, pop art, sexual promiscuity (my dears, how tedious) and, in 1963, the Profumo Scandal are all looked back on now as distinctive signs of remarkable social and political change as, of course, in the very short span of human life, they were. I must not allow my own extraordinary insight to prevent my recognizing that tiny pinpricks of experience must obviously assume absurdly disproportionate significance if they occur within a very limited time frame. But I will preamble, or possibly you will say ramble, no further, or I will lose your attention and I very much want you to stay with me to the end of this particular little journey back in time.

So, as I said, we are in the 1960's...A bright sunshiny spring morning in 1963, to be precise, and atoms of dust are floating in the brilliant rays that are lighting up the breakfast room of a handsome Queen Anne town house in Stanton Square, where a certain Mr. and Mrs. Mott are enjoying breakfast. The fragrant scent of coffee is in the air and Mr. Mott is spreading a crisp slice of toast with golden butter and succulent orange marmalade. Mrs. Mott is reading the newspaper, with a frown furrowing her brow and a grim expression of displeasure compressing her lips.

'Well really,' she says, with a rising intonation of outrage, her eyes fixed in fury on the newsprint in front of her.

Mr. Mott swallows a mouthful of toast rather too hastily and nearly chokes on some crumbs that have gone down the wrong way. Coughing, and with his eyes watering, he directs a look of dismayed inquiry at his wife. Mrs. Mott is an impressive woman by anybody's standards. She has a handsome face, a stately bosom and a purposeful no-nonsense manner. Mr. Mott is a more uncertain soul. Slight of build, rumpled of appearance and with a suggestion of gentle misgiving in his demeanour. Mr. Mott wears the skirts in the partnership and his good lady the trousers.

'What is it, dear?' he ventures.

'What isn't it, more like,' rages Mrs. Mott. 'Nowadays it's all just one vile piece of human villainy after another, so far as I can see. I knew how it would be the minute they allowed that disgusting book of Mr. Lawrence's to be published.'

Mr. Mott here tries to look as if he has never read Lady Chatterley's Lover and doesn't know what his wife is talking about.

'And now we have our Secretary of State for War, no less, embroiled in some sort of squalid scandal or other and imperilling all our lives in the process. We'll all be blown to pieces by the Russians before we can turn round. How Mr. Profumo could get himself involved with a showgirl is beyond me. Never mind one who, at the same time, is engaged in some sort of sordid liaison with a soviet naval attaché. It's all denied, of course.' She shudders expressively as her eyes fall on a particularly alluring news photograph of the showgirl in question, the beautiful Miss Keeler, and a finely tuned ear might detect a note of envy in the voice with which she then adds, 'I can't see what makes men lose their wits over her in such a way. She's nothing special, after all.'

Mr. Mott leans over and steals a glance at the photograph of the beautiful Miss Keeler and thinks that she looks very special indeed.

'I remember a time,' continues Mrs. Mott, 'when politicians upheld all the finest qualities of human nature and led the country by example.'

'Oh, I don't think they ever did that, my dear,' Mr. Mott is unable to prevent himself from saying.

'Don't talk nonsense, Charles. Of course they did. At any rate they didn't drag us all into the filth and the mire. Next they'll be trying to convince us that dung heaps smell sweet and that weeds should be left to flourish unchecked.' Mrs. Mott is a keen gardener and considers this piece of sarcasm particularly telling. Its stringency pleases her and puts her in a better frame of mind.

'Anyway, Charles, we won't waste time on the subject for there are far more agreeable things to think about and I want to show you my latest ideas for the rose trees and for the planting of the annuals. There are barely three months till the competition, you know.'

Every year, on a day towards the middle of June, the gardens of Stanton Square are open to the public and this year, for the first time, there is to be a competition and a prize awarded to the best garden. Mrs. Mott is determined to win it.

She puts aside her newspaper and, fetching her ground plan for the bedding plants, lays it on the breakfast table, and husband and wife are poring over it in amicable silence when a crashing and grinding noise outside in the street, shatters their concentration and makes Mrs. Mott rush to the window.

'I knew it,' she says, her good humour dispelled in an instant, 'it's those appalling new people next door. How long do they think we're going to put up with this racket? You'll have to go and speak to them Charles.'

Mr. Mott joins his wife at the window and is peering out disconsolately into the street, where rubble and enormous branches of dead trees and other garden detritus are being piled onto a lorry, when a little red Austin mini pulls up at the kerb and a young man with tousled brown hair climbs out.

'There he is now,' exclaims Mrs. Mott with triumph, '...and his silly wife. Whatever is she wearing?' A slender girl with a blonde fringe has just run down the steps of the house next door and is throwing her arms round the young man standing on the pavement. They turn and, hand in hand, go back into the house.

'Go and talk to them Charles,' instructs Mrs. Mott.

'I really don't see how I can, my dear, and in any case I thought you were so pleased when that house was finally sold and it and the garden saved from wrack and ruin.'

'That was before I knew what they were going to do to the place. Now I wish that dear old Professor Cunningham still lived there.'

Professor Cunningham had lived in No. 10 Stanton Square for as long as memory could recall. A reclusive intellectual, he had generally been locked away in his study with his books, his own most famous work being a lengthy academic tome entitled, People and Pests Through the Ages. His neighbours, though ever on the lookout, only ever caught very rare sightings of him and, year after year, the house had become more and more neglected and the garden more and more overgrown until, one day, the Professor had decided that, his research being completed, he now deserved the luxury of permanent seclusion from all forms of human knavery, destruction and folly – and died. The house had then lain empty until, some five months previously it had been bought by the modern young couple, Robert and Celia Haydon, who were quickly becoming the bane of Mrs. Mott's life.

When Robert and Celia moved in they had employed an architect to turn the elegant Queen Anne rooms into the open-plan space that was an essential requirement for any aspiring young professional couple in 1960's London. The architect had informed his innocent young clients that he wanted 'to open up bold panoramas within the house while, at the same time, preserving the existing spatial ratio of the dimensions. Clean lines, clear design,' and they had watched meekly as Queen Anne fireplaces and fine oak panelling were wrenched from the walls and hurled into the street. Mrs. Mott had also watched this pillage, though anything but meekly, from her vantage point at the breakfast room window. She had felt like slamming up the sash and shrieking out into the street, 'You BARBARIANS. Don't you know that you're supposed to protect everything that's lovely, not smash it to pieces?'

Today, however, Robert and Celia have an appointment with their landscape gardener and it is he whom they are hurrying into the house to receive. His knock is heard shortly afterwards and he is shown directly into the sitting room where newly fitted sliding plate glass doors open onto the tangled undergrowth that was once Professor Cunningham's garden. Clearance work is already well under way.

All the houses on that side of Stanton square open onto gardens at the back, which in turn open onto a narrow lane, and everything that is, at present, being cleared away is hauled through this lane and then loaded onto a lorry at the front of the house. The self-same lorry that causes Mrs. Mott such distress.

The landscape gardener has found his young clients as susceptible to suggestion as did the architect and, today, he presents them with his finished designs. 'We want to create not so much a garden, in the old recognized English sense of the word,' he explains with contemptuous dismissal, 'but rather to make an outdoor room, a paved space, a patio where, in the centre of London, you will have an illusion of southern skies and Mediterranean sunshine.' Robert and Celia are enchanted and only hope that there will be enough time to have everything ready for the Open Gardens Day in June and anxiously calculate how long they will need to realize their plans for their own little plot of earth under northern skies.

So the spring days lengthen as that earth spins in space and, tilting on its axis, turns March into April and April into May; and the gardens of numbers 8 and 10 Stanton Square draw in the renewed light and warmth of the sun. Work continues apace and, in the intervals between labouring on her own garden Mrs. Mott monitors the progress of the work next door, through one of her back bedroom windows. Horror and disbelief are her prevailing sensations. 'They're turning it into some kind of outsize back yard, so far as I can see,' she mutters to herself, in real distress. 'Not content with vandalizing the house, they have to set about wrecking the garden as well. Really, we don't have to wait for anybody else to destroy the country for we can do it perfectly well ourselves.' She can hardly bring herself to speak to her new neighbours whenever she meets them and is angry with her husband for being less angry than herself. And when, in an incautious moment, he tries to plead for her neighbours and lessen their offence by saying mildly, '"Striving to better, oft we mar what's well," my dear. King Lear, you know,' she replies, with great heat: 'Don't quote Shakespeare at me, Charles. If it comes to that, "fools and villains make of earth, a hell," which puts the whole thing in a nutshell, as far as I'm concerned. Really, you can be so pompous sometimes.'

Robert and Celia have some idea of the disquiet their alterations are causing by the frostiness that chills all their attempts to be friendly, but they are young and optimistic and naïve in their perceptions and try not to be troubled by any encounter with such old ideals and precepts as they find embodied in Mrs. Mott, so continue with their own plans undeterred.

Before anyone can believe it, the sun is once again shining from a June sky. Once again Mr. and Mrs. Mott are enjoying breakfast in their sunny breakfast room. Once again Mr. Mott is munching on toast and marmalade and sipping fragrant coffee and, once again, Mrs. Mott is reading the morning paper. This time she is reading with some satisfaction that Mr. Profumo has confessed that he has misled the House and lied in his previous testimony concerning Miss Keeler and that he is resigning his Cabinet position as well as his Privy Council and parliamentary membership. 'I should hope so too,' remarks Mrs. Mott, giving the pages an indignant shake. The paper does not, of course, report that Mr. Profumo will spend the rest of his life trying to ease suffering in the poorest parts of London. However Mrs. Mott is satisfied that national security has not been irredeemably compromised and that, whatever else is happening to England, it is, for the time being at least, safe from a nuclear explosion. As to permanent peace of mind on that score, she feels that it was dealt a fatal blow, some eight months previously, by the Cuban Missile Crisis.

Mr. Mott suspects the cause of his wife's indignation and has just decided that silence is the safest response to it, when there is a tentative little knock on the front door. Mrs. Mott wonders fretfully, 'who that can be?' and putting down her paper and pushing back her chair goes to open the door herself. She finds, to her astonishment, that her young neighbour, Celia, is standing on the doorstep.

'I'm so sorry to bother you at this hour of the morning,' says Celia shyly, 'but Robert and I are going to spend a few days with my parents and we've something we'd like to ask you before we go.'

Mrs. Mott's surprise is by no means lessened on hearing this, but she asks her young neighbour into the breakfast room, where Mr. Mott rises courteously to his feet and offers her coffee. Celia refuses the coffee with the plea that she 'really mustn't stay' and nervously gets straight to the purpose of her call.

'It's just that, as you obviously know, Robert and I have been making quite a lot of changes to our house and garden.'

'Indeed,' says Mrs. Mott shortly.

Mr. Mott looks uncomfortable.

'Yes well,' continues Celia, trying not to get flustered, 'when all the clearing work was being done on the garden, the men discovered a very old sundial hidden under an absolute mountain of ivy and stuff – I suppose it must have belonged to old Professor Cunningham. At first we didn't know what we should do with it, because the landscape gardener said it would look quite incongruous in our own garden.' Here she feels slightly discomfited by noticing that Mrs. Mott has put on her spectacles and is glancing once more over the paper, in rather a pointed way.

'And anyway' – in a rush – 'Robert says that what the sundial needs is a really beautiful garden, like your own, to stand in – we get little glimpses of it from our back bedroom window, you know – and Robert says, if you would like to come and have a look at it, the sundial I mean, and if you feel it would look nice in your garden, he could wheel it round in a barrow and help you put it wherever you'd like it to go.'

Mrs. Mott is nonplussed. She feels as if she has put on her armour for battle and her adversary has planted a kiss on her visor and begged her to sit down and make herself comfy.

Mr. Mott finds himself in the unusual position of having to speak instead of his wife.

'My dear girl,' he says, genuinely touched, 'we couldn't possibly take advantage of such generosity. You must keep the sundial yourselves.'

'No, really' Celia insists, 'we'd like you to have it. Won't you at least come and have a look at it?'

Mrs. Mott is actually longing to see the sundial and also to get a proper look at the new garden. The oblique glimpses of it through her upstairs window, with which she has had to content herself till now, have become frustrating. So, with an appearance of reluctance, she agrees to go next door.

Robert is waiting to greet them and the four of them make their way through the house, Mrs. Mott averting her eyes in affronted silence, from the desecration she knows she must otherwise see around her. They go into the sitting- room and through the 'absolutely frightful' (Mrs.

Mott's silent indictment of the sliding, plate glass doors) to
the patio garden at the back of the house. Here Mrs. Mott
does allow herself to look about her and is surprised, and
not altogether pleased, to find that now she is actually in it,
the new garden has a quite definite attraction all of its own.
Small paving stones pattern and cover the whole area that at
one time had been a lawn and white, round pebbles
measure its borders. Troughs and tubs are planted with
ferns and ivies, with hostas and dwarf cypresses and with
bay and lavender and there are pots of red and pink and
white geraniums making bright patches of colour. Water
splashes from a fountain and dimples the surface of a small
pool.

Mr. Mott is eager to admire what his wife will not.

'Well, this is lovely,' he says, looking around him with
delight, 'and it has quite a Mediterranean feel. I'd scarcely
know I was in England.'

Robert hears this praise with silent pleasure and, after a
little pause, glances at Mrs. Mott and says, 'But now come
and see the sundial.' He leads them to a still unreclaimed
part of the garden, where the dial has been covered in some
old sacking and stands tucked away in a corner. He pulls off
the sacking with an exaggerated flourish, and Mrs. Mott
gives a quite audible gasp.

'Oh, but it's absolutely lovely. Really and truly lovely,'
and turning to Celia says, in a voice that is almost gentle.
'You mustn't dream of parting with anything so beautiful.'

The sundial, made of soft-coloured stone, weathered
and smoothed by the centuries, is indeed lovely. The
pedestal is covered in tenderly wrought carvings of flowers
and birds and butterflies and these carvings also decorate
the rim of the dial. Roman numerals are set into its face and
around them are engraved the words of a motto, which Mr.

Mott, peering at the letters so closely that his nose nearly touches them, reads aloud:

This dial here marks ye London garden's hour,
By which reveals each season's leaf and flower.
Its shadow shows when weeds and thorns appear
To stunt good growth and damage year by year,
And indicates in sunlight how brief ye precious time,
To ['what's this word? Oh, yes. Love.'] to love and tend
    and treasure, thy fragile blooms and mine,
Prize Time.

Mr. Mott straightens himself up again and reflects, rather doubtingly, 'Well it's a charming sentiment at any rate.'

But Mrs. Mott's delight in the sundial is so obvious that Robert is emboldened to insist that it must at least be 'tried out' in the garden next door. So, wrapped protectively once more in its sacking, it is loaded onto a wheelbarrow and trundled down the lane and through the back garden gate of number 8 Stanton Square. And here Mrs. Mott, who has been at the forefront of the little procession, stands proudly to one side and lets her garden speak for itself. Celia whispers, 'Oh, how exquisite,' and Robert, without saying a word, rests his wheelbarrow on the ground and feels somehow that he should do more than simply stand and gaze and marvel.

For Mrs. Mott's London garden is telling, through the delicate flowers that grow there, how precarious and uncertain is its cultivated beauty.

Roses and honeysuckle, sweet pea and jessamine clamber over trellis and tumble over arches. Pear and plum and apple trees, their blossom now turning into budding fruit, are carefully trained against mellow brick walls that soak up the sunshine. In the flower beds that border the lawn all the favourite old-fashioned flowers with lovely sounding names are massed together in graceful profusion for their scent and shape and colour. Gilly flowers and hollyhocks, delphiniums and foxgloves, meadowsweet and ladysmock, daisies and carnations, mignonette and larkspur, heartsease and periwinkle, lupin and lavender, all in their season turn their faces to the sun. And the lawn itself, so soft and smooth and green, seems to be waiting, in complete serenity, for the sundial which is about to be placed in its very centre.

A week later Open Gardens Day dawns bright and sunny in Stanton Square. A marquee has been erected in the communal garden belonging to the square where a brisk trade is done all day in tea and home made cakes, lemonade and ice cream. A team of gardening grandees has been invited to judge the gardens and a solemn-looking representative from the Royal Horticultural Society to present the prizes

By late afternoon a crowd has gathered round a small platform, which has been erected in front of the marquee. The prize winner is just about to be announced.

'The gardens are all so very beautiful,' intones the solemn-looking representative, pronouncing his R's as W's with the help of a crackling microphone, 'that we have found it extremely difficult to decide upon where to award the first prize.' He flicks at the microphone with his finger, in an attempt to stop it crackling. 'In fact we have found it so difficult that we have concluded the only thing to do is to award the prize jointly, and we feel that the two gardens we have chosen illustrate perfectly the wonderful continuum of faith and hope, against the odds, that gardening has always inspired through the centuries.' The microphone suddenly emits a loud screech and the solemn-looking representative starts violently and takes a wild swipe at the air with his notes. But, recovering himself quickly, he resumes with increased solemnity. 'For us, the garden of Mr. And Mrs. Mott seems to safeguard all the best beloved traditions in the cultivating of our soil that we all treasure and hold in our hearts, while the garden, or courtyard, of Robert and Celia Haydon challenges and inspires us with new ideas and visions and represents, in its different way, the bold acceptance of a rapidly changing and, I'm sorry to say, seemingly more dangerous world.' He draws breath and eyes the microphone as if he suspects that it is going to give another screech but, since it merely continues crackling, he is able to conclude with unimpaired dignity, 'a world where, more than ever perhaps, we may need our cultivated gardens to provide us with a gentle refuge from the fears and uncertainties of the future and – if I may borrow the words of that keen gardener, Mr. Cowper, nearly two hundred years ago – "from the rank and overbearing race of weeds, noisome and ever greedy to exhaust the impoverished earth."'

That evening Mrs. Mott carries her rosette carefully home, relieved that all her efforts in planting and protecting have not been in vain and that her garden has been valued as it ought. Her feelings towards Robert and Celia are softened, accordingly, into a state of suspended hostilities and the hidden romance in her soul that has enabled her to grow so beautiful a garden even allows her to ponder on the whimsical notion of permanent ceasefire. At bedtime she is moved to giving Mr. Mott a kiss on his forehead before climbing into bed where she pulls up the covers and sleeps soundly all night long. Her dreams are only sweet ones concerning delightful accounts of her own beautiful garden, which she hopes to read in the local newspaper. She has ordered it to be delivered in plenty of time for breakfast the following morning.

★ ★ ★

And there, my dear people, with Mrs. Mott's slumbers, my little story ends and we can leave the London of 1963 behind us and return, once again, to this beautiful hall in the year 2006 and to a world where you find change taking place all around, at a speed that leaves many of you breathless and where danger seems to darken the sky more threateningly than ever. As for myself, I am afraid that my future is no more certain than your own. I have my first democratically elected Mayor, who isn't to everybody's taste, and an amount of bad-tempered crowding on my roads and pavements, which is to nobody's taste. Profumo flavoured scandals are eaten with breakfast every day of the year, and much more unsavoury fare besides, for the appetite grows by what it feeds on and wholesomeness was ever subject to ridicule. If you were to ask for my opinion of the present incumbents of my Houses of Parliament, I should feel obliged to tell you that I prefer not to speak of them at all. But fear, violence, treachery, destruction, political scheming, sophistical manipulation, jiggery-pokery and gobbledy-gook are ever in my midst, as they ever have been and ever will be. Only now a silent surveillance is ominously watching all.

My vast progeny increases until I begin to wonder, like many another woman, if I can cope with the size and demands of my brood, and every fond mother amongst you will understand the difficulty of upholding the need for curbs and restraints – without which ear-splitting pandemonium ensues. My instincts, which happily are admirable, make me long to succour the people and plants and ideas, which have always been drawn to me from every corner of the world yet, until cloning is perfected, there is only one of me and, astonishing though my capabilities may be, they are by no means inexhaustible. For everybody's sake, however, I hope that it will always be in my power to sustain the life which has been entrusted to my care. I consider compassion to be one of the finest of my qualities and existence without it would be terrible indeed.

Amongst my gardeners talk now turns on the possibility of growing olive trees and fig trees, oranges and vines in a hotter London soil though, for the time being, I am thankful to say, I am still regularly presented with posies of flowers, rather than baskets of olives (even when accompanied by a gin and Dubonnet, I am not at all keen on olives, especially the stuffed ones. But that is by the bye). I am told that I remain exceedingly beautiful and naturally I take a feminine pride in the fact, for I like to think that I am not defined mainly by my matriarchal role. It is a rare woman who does think so. No woman does.

But beauty and femininity provide no safeguards at all and catastrophes both of man and nature threaten me on every side. 'So what's new?' I hear somebody at the back of the hall cry out. Was that you sir? The overheated-looking gentleman, troubled with hiccups. Yes, you there, in the baseball cap turned the wrong way round. What's new indeed, sir. I am glad you have been attending. In my experience, so far as human behaviour is concerned, Absolutely Nothing. Not even heckling. But, at the same time, I am obliged to observe that the threat to my earthly existence seems greater now than ever before and, if I am spared a cataclysm of man's making, then I pray, that in the event of a deluge of natural disaster, such as is excitedly forecast, that my flood barriers and defences will hold and that the culminating heaven-bourn second may yet be many centuries away. But ultimately, my dear souls, like the sun, moon and stars, it is there for us all. I like to think, however, that a celestial Happiness is waiting for you as it, most assuredly, is for me. Dear heart alive, there is quite enough present gloom around, I should hope, without conjuring up more, in prospect.

In the meantime, spring is here again and my public parks and squares and gardens are magically renewed by the mysterious universal force of life. Dusty little back yards show green shoots of hope and in window boxes all over the city the first tiny tender spears quicken and stir and push their way through the dark earth and reach for the light.

People, your good selves included perhaps, will soon be flocking to the gardens of the Royal Horticultural Society and crowding the pathways of the Chelsea Flower Show. The seeking and the striving go on without pause, the clamouring for change, the jostling for gain, the scuffling for power, the squabbling for prizes. And all the while, amidst the uproar and in words that make no sound, the sundial in a London garden still says:

To love and tend and treasure, thy fragile blooms and mine, Prize Time.

And now, my dear people – dear children I had almost said, for so you seem to me – I believe that our own time this evening is nearly at an end and I hear the chimes of Big Ben striking the hour. It only remains for me to thank you all for your rapt attention – especially you, sir, the heckling gentleman with hiccups at the back of the hall. It has been a great pleasure to appear before you, in this way, as the Spirit of London and to talk to such an appreciative audience. May you always take such delight in listening and in learning; as well from the old sweet stories of long ago, as from the wisdom and experience made visible in me. But I can illuminate no further, for the closing moment is really upon us. The chairperson to my left has just asked me to remind you all that tea and buns will be served in the vestibule. I, unfortunately, will not be able to join you there. Those good, guardian angels, my security men are apparently getting anxious that some further skulduggery might be afoot and want to bundle me away to safety.

Birdsong

- Stella Robbins -

F or him, city life had always held something of the
horror of nightmare. The crowds, the smells, the filth,
the noise. The terrible noise. But now here the old man
was, on this sunny Saturday afternoon, in his own little
country garden, with no sounds to disturb his peace but the
pure singing of a blackbird on the topmost branch of a
beech tree and the sweet trilling of a wren in the hazel edge
nearby. Truly, 'the flowers appear on the earth and the time
of the singing birds is come,' the old man thought
contentedly, as he lay back in the summer softness and
closed his eyes.

He was dozing gently when the quiet and the calm
were blasted asunder as the thundering roar of a motorbike
shattered the air and pulverized birdsong, assaulting
tranquillity with a violence like physical attack.

The old man got up and walked down his garden to the
gate at the end of a little meadow and saw the motorbike
roaring round the perimeter of the field below, gouging the
banks and tearing deep gashes in the ground with the brutal
force of its wheels. The rider must have seen the old man,

for the motorbike swerved suddenly and, racing diagonally across the field, then thundered to a halt in front of the gate. The huge machine pounded and throbbed and the sun glinted on the black helmet of the rider as he revved the engine again and again. Even before the old man spoke, he knew it was useless to say anything. And the menace from the rider was palpable as he yowled and whooped and hollered:

'Fuck off, old man. Just fuck off.'

It was pointless to go back to his garden so the old man got into his car and drove to the coast, a few miles distant and sat on the shingle, in the salty spray, listening to the sounds of the sea.

The following Saturday the performance was repeated with no variation and the Saturday after that the old man didn't even attempt to sit in his garden. He just drove to the coast, to the call of the waves and the cry of the gulls and the deep unfathomable soundings of the sea.

On the fourth Saturday rain was descending in torrents, so it would be impossible for anyone to be outside, but there was an old film the old man wanted to see on his television and he could spend an afternoon lost in nostalgia. Yet he was barely settled in his favourite armchair before the roar of the motorbike invaded the room and, shattering sanctuary, made the film on television inaudible.

It was too wet to go to the coast, so the old man got into his car and drove to the nearest town and did his shopping. When he returned in the evening the house was quiet once more and the old man unwrapped a little bunch of flowers that he had bought and arranged them in a jug of water. Then he put the rest of his shopping away in a cupboard, keeping out two strawberry cupcakes, which he ate with a mug of hot tea, before taking himself slowly off to bed.

The next Saturday was fine again but, of course, the old man made no attempt to sit in his garden. He merely waited, tremulously, for the roar of the motorbike to begin and when it did he felt his heart falter in fear. But he went to his cupboard and taking out a bulky, beautifully wrapped parcel that he had bought in town, the week before, struggled with it down the garden, through the long grass to the gate that led to the field. If you can't beat 'em, join 'em, he thought sadly, as he opened the gate, and yet he didn't see how he was ever to feign an interest in the motorbike or appease its rider.

The air was now thundering with a force and brutality of sound and a second later the huge machine was throbbing and pounding in front of the old man and he felt more powerfully than before the threat and menace from its rider. But this time the old man made no appeals for peace, nor asked for any consideration. He even tried to look friendly as he unwrapped his parcel with shaking hands and, proffering it to the rider, pulled the trigger. The noise was terrible. Deafening the ears of the old man.

'Fuck off, lad,' he said, as he turned and walked away, 'Just fuck off.'

When he got back to his garden the air was filled with silence. There was nothing but silence. The blackbird and the wren had flown away. Not a note of their music remained. The roar of the motorbike had only muted their song, but the blast from the shotgun had stilled it forever.

Stella Robbins

Grizelda Tyler

Grizelda Tyler was born in Scotland and spent most of her childhood in London, Edinburgh and Aberdeenshire. After graduating, she went to live permanently in London where she worked as a social worker. She then had three daughters and became involved with local community projects and charities. In 1990 in response to a growing interest in food and its provenance she started an organic co-operative with friends and neighbours. In 1995 she moved with her husband and daughters to Aylsham, Norfolk.

Grizelda has always had a desire to write and follow in her father's footsteps. When she was a child he had written fairy stories in which she, her brother and elder sister had all had starring roles. Whilst writing for herself Grizelda has never had the courage to hope to be published until attending a creative writing course in Aylsham.

Grizelda Tyler

The Plan
- Grizelda Tyler -

Late November 1912. The dark Scandinavian winter had settled in. The coldness was intensified by the gathering dusk. The houses in the riverside terrace had seen better days; the, once bright, paint was peeling from the woodwork, the gardens were mostly unkempt, in keeping with their residents. Electric light had not yet reached this part of Gothenburg and the light thrown out by the gas lamps was gloomy, colluding with the general air of despair. On a low brass bed in the first floor bedroom of one of these houses was a beautiful young woman. She lay curled up, her long winter dressing gown wrapped tightly around her, her feet encased in thick woollen socks. The light from a small oil lamp shone on her blond hair, deep grey eyes and sensual lips. Sighing, she turned onto her side and gazed at the room. Even in the darkness every nook and cranny was familiar to her. It was cold and depressing but it was her refuge, the physical manifestation of her inner battles; the blue silk cushions epitomised her ambition, the faded wooden furniture the prison that threatened to entomb her. She could feel the familiar rising of the fingers of resentment and contempt like two serpents fighting to escape. In an effort to keep them at bay she rose from the bed and placed a small piece of wood on the dying embers of the fire. For a couple of brief seconds a warm yellow flame lit up the room, exposing its air of shabby gentility. Picking up a candlestick, Anna lit the candle and placed it on the table. She looked at her reflection in the mirror. A light knock on the door interrupted her reverie and her mother walked in clutching a small leather box.

'Anna darling, it's so cold in here. Would you like me to fetch some more wood?'

'It won't make any difference. The wind howls through the window and the curtains
aren't thick enough to keep it out.'

Anna gazed at her mother. Karen Goranson was a tall, elegant woman, a look borne out more by her bearing than her clothes. Her attractive fine boned face was lined and
drawn, her stooped shoulders a testimony to subjugation.

She's been crying again. Why doesn't she just leave him, I would have. 'Where's Papa?'

'In the sitting room.'

'What doing nothing as usual, I suppose'

Karen ignored her daughter's complaints: there really was little else she could do. Sitting down on the bed, she opened the small leather box and withdrew a delicate, diamond encrusted bracelet and a pair of earrings.

'Mama, they are so beautiful,' gasped Anna and smiling at her mother, added : ' I never knew you had these. How have you managed to keep them hidden?' She took them from her mother's outstretched hand and held them in the candlelight; the jewels glistened and flirted in the flame.

'Well, I haven't had much opportunity to wear them recently, so they have been kept in a safe place, and it will be such a grand occasion tonight, you must have them'.

An overwhelming feeling of pity hit Anna, and, crossing over to where her mother sat she threw her arms around her neck and hugged her. Karen willingly gave herself up to her daughter's embrace and affection, but their rare moment of closeness was interrupted by a bad tempered bellow from below.

'Is the blasted girl so incompetent she cannot even dress herself for this charade? I need you down her immediately, Karen.'

Biting her lip to stop the torrent of abuse she knew would come, she closed the door behind her mother's fast disappearing back. She resumed her place in front of the mirror to apply her make up. She did so with extreme care, her hand steady and skilful. After a few moments she paused and gazed critically at her reflection. She was beautiful. She knew she was beautiful. She could see it in the way men looked at her and women stared at her with jealousy. She didn't care; her beauty was her escape route. She drew back from the mirror and stood up. Walking over to the dress hanging on the wardrobe, she took off her dressing gown and slipped the pale pink silk over her head. She allowed the rich cool material to fall slowly down her body, caressing her breasts and hinting at the long outline of her legs. The initial impression was one of purity but the semi-obscured slit from demure neckline to belly button implied something far more sensual. Opening her mother's small leather box and gently removing the diamonds, she put them on.

Facing the wardrobe mirror and standing on tiptoes to see how her legs looked, she was pleased with what she saw.

She slipped on the gold high - heeled shoes, picked up her stole and walked out of the room. Before she reached the bottom of the stairs, her stole was wrapped tightly around her, obscuring the top half of her body. Her mother quickly came out of the kitchen in response to Anna's heels hitting the bare hall floor.

'Darling, you look wonderful.'

'Anna, the Hanson's are here, don't keep them waiting'. Her father's hard caustic voice sent her hurrying out of the house and into the waiting carriage.

Anna and her friend Britta Hanson entered the main ballroom of the Grand Hotel.

Every light was blazing and the music of the Gothenburg Orchestra filled the air with the sense of occasion. Every one of import in the city and the surrounding area was there. The feeling of curiosity was palpable. As the girls moved into the centre of the room, Anna was conscious of eyes being turned her way. She walked slowly across the brightly lit room, well aware that Greville Niels had seen her, conscious of his eyes following her. He was certainly much better looking and more powerful in the flesh than in his description in the papers. Reaching the table with the champagne, she picked up a glass and, turning, saw that Greville was making his way towards her. Looking straight at him, she engaged his eyes.

One lady, slightly grander than others touched her neighbour's arm. ' Lisa, look there is the Hanson girl, but who is the one in the pink? She is gorgeous but arrogant.'

'That's Karen Goranson's daughter,' her neighbour confided, 'you know, Karen Hamilton, that was.'

'Wasn't it Carl Goranson who lost all his money in the 1900 crash and then took to drink?'

'Do you know, my dear, I think you are right - no wonder we haven't seen her before.

How on earth can she come into society with that sort of history?'

'But she has breeding. After all, her mother is a Hamilton.'

'Not much use if your father is a drunkard and a failure.'

'Poor girl, how awful for her.'

'Oh, I don't think she needs your sympathy- she seems perfectly capable of looking after herself- look she has already caught the eye of Greville Niels.' Both ladies turned to look at the tall, good looking man watching the girls.

'Yes, but you know his reputation.'

'The young Miss Goranson doesn't look to me as if she would mind too much about his reputation.'

'Marianne, really.'

Greville was bored. He couldn't abide these trips to the sticks; the food was awful, the beds uncomfortable, and as for the people, fawning bourgeoisie, the women far worse than the men- heaven forbid that he should have to spend an evening with one of them.

However, this young lady in the pink silk might be worth pursuing. She looked as though she might be an interesting distraction.. She was certainly beautiful, looked intelligent and slightly haughty- definitely a challenge to be investigated.

'Good Evening Miss?'

'Goranson.'

'Allow me to introduce myself.'

'That will not be necessary. I know who you are Herr Niels.'

Greville smiled.' Well you are well informed.'

'I have always believed it pays to be prepared. Actually everyone in Gothenburg has talked of little else; ever since it was known that you were due to come here.'

'How very tedious for you, Miss Goranson.'

'Oh no I don't think so. It has engendered enormous curiosity which, from an observer's perspective, never fails to alleviate boredom, especially when satisfied.'

'And has it been?'

'Oh yes, I think so.'

'How, may I ask?'

'Well I already know an immense amount about you. The deductive abilities of the good ladies of Gothenburg are renowned; I am very surprised you were not warned of their enormous tenacity!' Anna smiled and raised her glass to her lips.

Greville swept his eyes over her. On close inspection she was very striking. He took in the slender figure and the provocative sensuality of her dress.

An aide appeared and touched his elbow. 'Herr Niels, it is time for your speech.'

'I am coming.' Looking at Anna, he said, 'Miss Gornason I do hope you are not going to disappear like Cinderella at midnight. I should like to continue our discussion.'

'I do not have a Fairy Godmother, and as you can see no glass slippers either.'

He smiled and turned to follow his aide. Almost immediately, he returned. 'Shall we say lunch here tomorrow, 12.45?'

★ ★ ★

The morning was bright and cool. Gothenburg was at its best. The sun sparkled off the water, the trees glistened white with the heavy frost. Anna's walk was light and optimistic; so far everything was going to plan. At precisely 1.00 she entered the Grand Hotel.

'Ah Miss Goranson, for a moment I thought you might have forgotten or found something more interesting to do.' Anna smiled and took Greville's outstretched hand. 'I don't think so.'

A waiter came to take her coat. 'Can I bring you a drink before luncheon, Madam?'

'A small aquavit.'

'And for you Sir?'

'Whisky.'

Greville placed a hand on Anna's back. He guided her to a table in the window, obscured by wooden panelling from the eyes of their curious fellow diners. Anna settled into her chair.

'Now Miss Goranson, yesterday I learnt that I have been the sole topic of conversation. I am extremely interested to know what your fellow citizens are saying. Please put me out of my misery.'

'Well Herr Niels.'

'Call me Greville.'

'Thank you. Well Greville. I must first debate with my conscience as to whether or not I should betray the confidences of the good people of Gothenburg, but I am by nature merciful, so I shall.' And with a smile playing about her lips, Anna continued.

'You are here to see if we are suitable for your next venture. You come from a distinguished family; your father was the Ambassador to London and your Uncle is a serving General- or was it a Bishop ?- there seems to be some technical dispute here!!'

'A General,' he replied, laughing. 'Do go on.'

'Are you sure?'

To his surprise Grevill was enjoying himself. He liked women of spirit.

'Yes.'

'You were born and went to school in Stockholm, but studied engineering at Lund.

However you chose not to follow the family tradition of army, navy or diplomatic corps but instead were seduced by the new area of film. Some say this was because of the beautiful women it attracted.' Anna paused and looked straight at him- he returned her gaze unflinchingly and, sipping his wine, said quietly, 'Do continue.'

'You are forty and live in Stockholm on your own. You have never married, although your name has been linked with several notable beauties.' Anna stopped at this point and,leaving a second of quiet, then continued. 'I am afraid after this it becomes less interesting. I cannot, of course, testify to its validity.' Anna was surprised at her brazenness but she judged that this fish was certainly interested in the bait.

'Well Miss Goranson. I have no information on your life at all. I do not even know your Christian name.'

'My life is singularly dull.'

'I do not believe that - an intelligent, ambitious and beautiful young woman like you. Tell me all. I am very curious'.

'I am 22. My name is Anna and I have always lived here in Gothenburg with my parents. I did well at school but was unsure of what I wanted to do with my life. I just know there has to be more to it than living here.'

'Have you ever been to Stockholm?'

'No.'

'Well, maybe I should give you the opportunity to widen your horizons.'

* * *

Anna slipped further down the large bed. The soft linen sheets were like velvet on her skin. Was it really only three months since she had left Gothenburg? It felt like a lifetime.

The image of her mother flashed through her mind. She had been so pleased when

Anna had told her she was going to work in Stockholm as an assistant to Greville Niels. She hadn't lied to her mother. She had just not told her everything. To date the optimistic plan she had hatched in her cold depressing bedroom in Gothenburg had turned out to be far more successful than she could have imagined. Greville had been wonderfully generous. The clothes, the jewels, the parties and his undivided attention when they were alone. She knew he was substantially older than her, but she was also aware that this gave her added attraction. Her reverie was interrupted by a gentle knock on the bedroom door and the housemaid telling her that Greville's secretary was waiting for her in the Salon.

'I won't be a minute, Louise. Please tell Franz Josef I will be there shortly.'

Anna leapt out of bed and throwing on a beautiful warm cashmere dressing gown hurried to the Salon.

'Good morning, Miss Goranson.'

'Good morning, Franz Josef. Have you a message for me from Herr Niels?'

'Yes, Miss Goranson.' He picked up his leather brief case and extracted a large letter which he handed to Anna.

'Herr Niels presents his compliments and asks that you have left this apartment by 5.00 this evening.'

'I do not quite understand. I thought Herr Niels and I were to dine at the Hogstraten this evening.'

'Herr Niels has had a change of plan and he no longer requires your services now or in the future. The contents of the envelope are to assist you in finding alternative accommodation.'

Biting her lip, Anna took the letter and left the Salon. When she reached the privacy of her own room she allowed herself to give vent to anger. Franz Josef must be wrong, it must be a joke, but on ripping open the envelope, she discovered it was not. How dare he. She was being bought off like a common whore-she had been naïve –she should have seen this as a possibility- she had been complacent and too optimistic about the future. This rejection was not part of her plan. She had never pretended to herself that she loved Greville, but it had been an arrangement she was happy to live with. Now she must gather her thoughts to protect her position. She packed whatever valuables she could find and left.

In the carriage on the way to the Station Anna counted the money. It was a substantial amount, but she would need more to survive the coming months. Two things were now essential. She had to maintain and increase her funds and put distance between herself and Greville. Anna sat in the Station Café assessing her skills, and where best she would be able to put them to use. She remembered that her mother had often talked of an elderly relation who lived in the North of Sweden at Ostersund. It was an industrial town and inaccessible, except by rail from November to April. This would suit her needs.

Going to the ticket office, she bought a single ticket.

★ ★ ★

The train crawled into Lund Station. Anna picked her way down the steep carriage steps onto the platform. Behind her, a kindly old man was carrying her suitcase.

'Thank you so much for your help,' Anna said, smiling, and stretching out her hand to grasp his.

'My pleasure completely, my dear. I do so hope that everything turns out for the best,' and, returning her smile, he gave a short bow and went on his way.

Standing alone on the platform, she did not feel despondent. On the contrary she experienced an enormous sense of relief. This was the right place to be. She beckoned to a porter, who picked up her case and led her to the front of the station and into a waiting carriage.

'Where to, Madam?' Anna searched in her handbag and, drawing out a small piece of paper, gave the driver the address.

This was the first time she did not have to search for lodgings. Her landlady in Uppsala had recommended her sister-in-law a Mrs Erickson, who ran a small lodging house off the main square. As the carriage moved off the full beauty of the old town became apparent. The late August sky was streaked with the red fingers of sunset, casting long shadows from the Cathedral spire and the old University buildings. The place seemed alive with activity and life, and this optimism transferred itself to Anna. Smiling to herself, she felt able to start to look forward to the future.

After a short drive, they stopped in front of an attractive wooded house and Anna alighted. The door was opened by a friendly grandmotherly woman who took Anna's hand and led her inside.

'You must be tired after your long journey my dear. Let me show you to your room.'

Physically she was exhausted. Since February she had been constantly on the move and this, with the ever present need for vigilance had taken its toll. She had been successful in the two aims she set herself before she left Stockholm all those months ago. She had put distance between herself and Greville and had increased her funds. In order to do the latter she had put herself and her unborn child at risk by using the threat of exposure of the pregnancy to extract monies from Greville. With attention to detail and careful planning she had managed to stay one jump ahead of his henchmen. It was necessary for the transfer of monies that he knew which town she was in, but he had never known where her lodgings were. She had always used a false name.

Now at last, here in Lund, she felt able to relax. The baby was due in a week and she had decided that as soon as she was able she would take her child and move abroad, away from her past and away from Greville.

Over the next few days, Anna rested and regained her strength, cosseted and cared for by Mrs. Erikson, for whom nothing was too much trouble. Indeed, it was she who called the carriage to take Anna to the Hospital, and it was she who was Anna's only visitor when Willhelm was born.

September and October were warm and sunny. They passed in a haze of intense contentment. Anna had never been so happy. For the first time in her life she felt complete. Her son was the centre of her being, her reason to live. She loved him with an all consuming passion.

In early November Anna received a letter from the bank asking her for an appointment in a couple of days. It was to discuss a minor problem with her account. At the appointed hour, Anna left her lodgings, leaving Willhelm in the care of Mrs. Erikson, and hurried to the Bank. On arrival, she gave her name to the clerk and went and sat in the waiting area. Picking up a discarded newspaper, her eye was caught by an article on film. Scanning it quickly, she soon found what she knew would be there: Greville's name. It was not, however, in connection with his latest enterprise, but rather it concerned his forthcoming marriage. Apparently, he was to be married to the daughter of one of the wealthiest men in Sweden. A man well known for applying his strict Lutheran principles, not only to his business, but also to his personal and family affairs. Her attention had been so deeply engaged, that she was initially unaware of the clerk calling her name.

' I am so sorry. I did not hear you.'

'That's alright Mrs Goranson, it is just that I only started here today and I have had some difficulty trying to track down the gentleman you have asked to see. It appears that we do not have anyone of that name in the Bank.'

'But that is ridiculous, you must have. Look, here is his letter.'

'I can assure you, Madam that we do not have this gentleman working here.'

Anna stared at him. The article about Greville's forthcoming wedding and the importance and position of the woman he was to marry hit her like a heavy blow to her stomach. She could now see it all. An intense panic gripped her like the talons of a vulture grasping its prey. She could hardly breathe, but she started to run. How could she have been so stupid. She had been so careful, but not careful enough. Just when she believed she was safe, he had struck.

As she ran up the steps to the front door, Mrs. Erikson opened it, smiling broadly.

'There you are at last. It was such a pity you weren't here. The only day you are out and your husband arrives.

He was so sorry you weren't in but so pleased to see Willhelm. He has taken him to the Park for a while, but I expect he will be back soon.'

Anna sank to the ground. She knew it was useless to wait.

★ ★ ★

It was late November again and the frosts were creeping up the dark, deserted streets of Gothenburg. Anna lay curled up on her bed, her long winter dressing gown wrapped tightly around her. There was no light in the room, only the cold shafts of moonlight falling through the window. She lay in a frozen state, eyes closed and lips moving in silent prayer. The intensity of the pain of loss was unbearable. After a while, stretching out her hand, she picked up the multi-coloured pram rug lying next to her. Hugging it to her, she breathed in the scent of Willhelm that it held. Tears streamed down her face, the full force of despair and grief tumbling out.

Nothing was left of him. Her baby, her little boy. Where was he now, who was he with, who was raining kisses on his beautiful blond curls, who would watch him take his first step, hear his first word, hug him better when he fell? Cascading through her mind, these thoughts tortured her, but she did not seek an escape for each one conjured a memory.

This was all she had left.

Anna knew she would never see her child again. She was dead from within and a cold impenetrable shield was wrapping itself around her like a cloak.

Daring to play the game, and believing she could win, had cost her her heart. Greville was the outright winner, and she the defeated foe.

Reality

- Grizelda Tyler -

I have to get off the train at Swineshead Bridge Station. And wait. Which I do.

It's cold, three o'clock in the afternoon and the mist is swirling off the flat fens. I wait.

What on earth am I doing here? I am here because of a phone call. I think it was a woman who called me. Her voice, or maybe his voice, was disguised. It was difficult to make out gender or age. So here I am, waiting, knowing nothing about the person I am waiting for.

The last few days seem to have affected my powers of judgement. This time last week I was boarding a London bound plane at Bangkok's new airport; the temperature was 80 F. I was relaxed and happy. I had just had two weeks travelling round Laos after finishing a gruelling three week assignment in Southern Thailand for the BBC. Now here I am in the freezing fens waiting for a stranger. My parents are in hospital in a coma after a serious assault in their own home. I am the main suspect. Apparently I was seen leaving their house shortly before they were discovered by a neighbour. It seems I even smiled and said hello to the neighbour. But I wasn't there I was 55,000 ft above Europe.

A small red mini draws into the station car park. It stops close to me. The driver opens the passenger window and leaning over calls out to me.

' Miss Stickels.'

'Yes, I am Janet Stickels.'

'Get in.'

I open the passenger door and get in. Here is the stranger who in the phone call assured me they have the answer to my present awful predicament. I must admit I am now feeling rather nervous, but at the same time I am compelled by an almost hysterical desire to resolve this ghastly situation. It is as though the very act of coming here to the Fens has opened a floodgate of desperation.

'I am sorry; I don't know your name'

'You do not need to know, Miss Stickels, just get in.'

She is wearing large dark glasses and a brown headscarf which combine to obscure most of her face. I can see a little of her profile but on no account would I be able to describe her. She is aware of me looking at her.

'The glasses are to protect my eyes; they are particularly sensitive so the glasses are not, as you obviously think, an affectation.'

'Oh no, I didn't think that at all. Is it hereditary?'

'Not as far as I know. Why do you ask?'

'Oh, it's only that my aunt has a similar condition.' I can feel her tensing and I want to move the conversation on as quickly as I can. I sit quietly trying to place her accent.

'You said on the phone that you had some information that might be helpful to me in resolving the attack on my parents.'

'Yes, I believe I do.' Her tone indicates that I should say nothing further until we reach our destination, wherever that might be. She puts the car into gear and we drive out onto the main road, heading towards Heckington Mill. There is very little traffic. The only car I see is the one that follows us out of the station car park having picked up the passenger who got off the same train as me. The weather is not improving, if anything the rain and mist are intensifying, making it gloomier and much harder to see. The car picks up speed and we travel about five miles before slowing to take a turning on the left into a clearing in the woods. The car park is empty. It's the sort of place used by dog walkers and ramblers. There is a map of the area on a notice board just before the path disappears into the trees. She stops the engine and turns towards me. She says nothing but looks straight at me, her eyes hidden by the black of her dark glasses.

'Perhaps,' I begin tentatively, 'you can tell me how you think you can help me.'

'All in good time, Miss Stickels. First there are things I need to know. How old are you?'

'Really this is ridiculous, I cannot see what relevance that can possibly have.'

'I don't care whether you think it has any relevance or not, just answer the question.'

'Alright. I am 44.'

'You have worked for the BBC for twenty years. Would you say you have had a good life?'

'Yes I do work for the BBC and I have worked for them for twenty years. And yes, I have been extremely fortunate in my life.'

'Are you married ?'

'No, I am divorced.'

'Have you got any children ?'

'Yes, One son.'

'And what about your parents, Miss Stickels ? Would you say you have a good relationship with them ? Did you have a happy childhood ?'

'Yes to all of that. Look is this really necessary?'

'It is very necessary, Miss Stickels and I have not finished yet. Do you have any brothers or sisters?'

'No, I am an only child.'

'Are you sure? Didn't you ever wonder why your parents didn't have more children?'

'No, I can't really say that I did. I never thought about it. I was just happy with Mum and Dad.'

'Oh, I am sure you were Miss Stickels. I am sure it was a very happy childhood without the problems of sibling rivalry.'

'Look, I simply do not understand where this is going.' I am feeling increasingly uncomfortable. ' Can't you just tell me what it is you know.'

'I am sure you would like to be let off the hook but even though it wasn't you, you are not going to be let off the hook. That would be too easy.'

'What do you mean too easy?'

The woman starts to undo her headscarf. I turn towards her. Her hair is brown, almost the same colour as mine. She takes off her large dark glasses and I am looking at myself.

'Oh my God ! Who the hell are you ?'

'Frightening is it? Makes you feel uncomfortable does it? You see you do have a sister after all, Janet. Well, where are your manners, a nicely brought up girl like you, well educated, intelligent, self confident, loved. A real little Miss Perfect. I am the one your beloved, or should I say our beloved, parents gave away. You see they didn't want me so they sent me to Australia. I dare say they believed the couple they gave me to would look after me, be kind to me, even love me, but they didn't. Instead they treated me like a slave from when I was tiny. And I am back to get my revenge. The look of horror on their faces when I started to hit them was worth waiting for. The destruction of their precious daughter Janet and her career in the BBC will be the icing on the cake. I have to admit I was half tempted to let them go on believing it was you, just like that stupid old woman next door did, but then I wouldn't have been fully revenged. So they know it was me and it was all their own fault.'

'How could you? I am sure they believed they were doing the right thing.'

'I don't care what they thought. Now get out of the car and let's get it finished.'

She opens her bag and takes out a small revolver.

'What are you going to do?' I try to keep my voice steady, unsuccessfully

'You don't really think I am going to let you survive do you? I thought a nice tasteful suicide would do the job. You can see the headlines – Miss Janet Stickels, successful BBC reporter, shoots herself after assaulting and badly injuring elderly parents- makes quite a good story, don't you think? Now get out of the car and put your hands on the roof.'

I do as I am told. Coming round beside me and pushing the nozzle of the gun into my back, grabs my elbow and makes me walk towards the path that leads into the trees. Suddenly she stops. She listens intently. There is some rustling in the leaves. It is difficult to see in the gloom. It is probably only some woodland animals. There is nobody around, no saviour on a white horse- this is it. I am going to die, killed by my own sister.

I am about five metres from the notice board when it seems to move. Simultaneously I am grabbed by a pair of strong hands and pulled from my sister's grasp. The wood is full of camouflaged policemen. It is over.

It's good to see my parents sitting in the comfort of their own home, bruises and all.

'Why on earth didn't you tell me?'

' It was never the right time and after a while it seemed for the best.'

'Well, it very nearly wasn't.'

Gloria Yeulet

Gloria Yeulet's great grandparents, originally from Poland, came to England around the start of the 20th century and settled in Croydon, Surrey, which is where Gloria was born. She moved to Norfolk in 1994 and now thinks of North Norfolk as her home. Apart from story writing, she also enjoys writing poetry and painting portraits. Her latest challenge is trying to learn to speak Mandarin.

Gloria Yeuler

Dead Lucky
- Gloria Yeulet -

M ary Metcalfe was seething.
At her husband Jack.

And the world in general as she lay on the NHS bed in the small ward. It was bad enough that she was ill and had to have this ghastly operation and be left with all these tubes and drips coming out of her arms and every orifice you could mention, let alone having to be in an NHS ward. It was all so demeaning. Her son Simon had tried to arrange for her to go into a private hospital but Jack had said it was too expensive. At least Simon tried, she thought, not like my useless lump of a husband who did nothing. He had no idea of how humiliated she would be if her friends at the golf club got to know of it. She would never live it down. And to top it all she was to be moved into the Council run nursing home at the end of her road to recuperate because it would be easier for Jack to visit her every day. Easier for Jack, oh yes, but what about me? My feelings obviously don't count. It's too awful to bear thinking about.

And that silly woman in the bed opposite is getting on my nerves-all smiles and gratitude to the doctors and nurses - I'll wipe that smile off her face.

'Nurse, Nurse, turn that awful television programme off. It's disturbing my rest.'

The woman looked sad and said something about it being her favourite programme-Good I'm glad I upset her - Why should I be the only one to be upset? Mary felt better, smiled to herself and allowed herself to think about all the other things she had done to those who crossed her or got on her nerves. Her daughter Molly had not spoken to her since she had demanded the return of the old furniture she had given her. Mary savoured the pleasure of then chopping it up while Molly watched. She had laughed at the look on Molly's face and it made her smile for years thinking about it, knowing that Molly had then put herself in debt to replace the furniture.

★ ★ ★

Alice Brown found it hard not to dislike the woman in the bed opposite. She knew the woman was very ill and tried to make allowances for her strange behaviour and attitude, not just to her, but also the nurses and doctors. Not long to go for me now she thought. This time tomorrow I will be sunning myself by the sea while I recuperate from my operation to remove one of my kidneys. Nurse Bridget had already removed Alice's tubes, drips and catheter.

'I now know what a cow feels like,' she said. 'It's like a set of bagpipes hanging down.'

Nurse Bridget laughed. 'Behave yourself, Alice. I'm going off duty now. I'll see you tonight'.

Alice felt great it was fantastic to be free to move about. She had a shower. Washed her hair. A nurse helped her into a fresh nightgown. She was now ready to face the world. Propped up with pillows, sitting in the easy chair next to her bed, she concentrated on ordering her dinner from the menu card.

Alice was startled to hear the woman in the bed opposite shouting for a nurse. Then, because the nurse did not arrive quickly enough for her, she threw her pillows onto the floor, which made her fall back and rendered her unable to sit up. The nurse picked up the pillows and propped her up again.

'Would you like to sit in the chair for a while?' she asked.

'No I wouldn't.'

'It will help with your recovery, you know, and stop you getting any problems with your chest. We don't want you getting pneumonia, do we?'

'I said no. Leave me alone. And don't keep eating my chocolates. No wonder you're so fat. What do you do? Wait for the patients to fall asleep and take their chocolates?'

'Now, now, Mary, you know that's not true, and it is unkind of you to say things like that.'

The nurse returned to her station.

Alice could not understand why Mary was being so awkward. Surely she wanted to get better? She padded over to her.

'Would you like me to order your dinner for you? They've got fish and chips, roast lamb or sausage and mash.'

'No. Just leave me alone.'

Alice padded back to her chair and saw Mary's husband Jack coming into the ward, as did Mary, who promptly closed her eyes and pretended to be asleep. He sat down on the chair next to her bed, armed with a bouquet of flowers, fruit, chocolates and her favourite 'Country Life' magazine, waiting for her to wake up. He liked to be early. Didn't want his wife to feel neglected during visiting hours. Goodness knows, she has been through a lot of pain, but hopefully now she will be on the mend and regain her strength once she has recovered from her operation. He thought the faded blue and yellow curtains and screen covers had seen better days and wondered if Mary would have something to say about that. She usually had quite a lot to say about the hospital and its lack of refined comforts that she would have liked.

Alice couldn't understand why Mary was pretending to be asleep. She felt sorry for her husband and said:

'Why don't you sit in the day room - there's newspapers and a television in there. You can get a cup of tea or coffee from the machine. Come on, I'll show you where it is and I'll come and get you when your wife wakes up.'

This infuriated Mary, who wanted Jack to feel embarrassed while he sat staring into space, not knowing quite where to look. Jack followed Alice, and Mary suddenly heard him say:

'Don't I know you? Yes I do. It's Alice Jones isn't it?'

Mary couldn't hear any more. They were out of earshot.

'Was Alice Jones. I'm Alice Brown now. My husband Jim died two years ago. I'm on my own now. I do remember you Jack. Gosh, all those years ago when we worked in the bookshop. You dreamed of writing a best seller-did you ever write your book?'

They walked into the day room.

'Fancy you remembering that. No I didn't. I made a half-hearted attempt but somehow life got in the way. You know how it is. Met Mary. Got married. Had two children, Simon and Molly. I'm a granddad now.'

'Why don't you try again now your children are grown up? It would be such a pity to waste your talent.'

'I might just do that - I'll let you know when I've got started. By the way, how do I contact you?'

'Well, for the next couple of months I'll be at the Cherry Trees Nursing Home in Cromer, just till I am strong enough to cope on my own. Anyway, I'll leave you now. I'll give you a call when your wife wakes up.'

★ ★ ★

Simon Metcalfe parked his car and reluctantly made his way through the rain to the hospital entrance. The past two weeks had dragged by. He missed his wife and children. He wanted to go home. He hated keep going backwards and forwards to the hospital. The horror of his first visit wafted over him as he recalled walking into the small, drab ward. Panic had overtaken him. He had stood in the middle of the ward, trying to recognise his mother. He didn't know which bed to go to. The patients all looked the same. All grey-haired old women whose personalities had been taken out and put in a glass of water with their false teeth. A nurse had come to his rescue and led him to his mother's bed. Since her operation, she had been moved to another equally drab ward. He was delighted to hear that her operation had been a complete success but worried about what her reaction would be to being moved to a Council run nursing home. Dad had resigned himself to her outbursts and tantrums and remained stoical. Simon wondered what he really felt but had never been able to find a chink in his armour.

'Don't worry, son, it's just her way.'

But Simon didn't like her way. Neither did his wife Doreen nor his sister Molly. Perversely she was a wonderful grandmother. Always had a stock of dressing up clothes for the children and was willing to be the audience for their impromptu plays and concerts. Heckling:

'Don't stand there like a dummy. Let's have some action.'

He smiled to himself, remembering that, and was relieved to find that his Dad was already in the ward when he arrived. It would make his visit bearable.

★ ★ ★

Nurse Bridget made herself a cup of tea and settled down at the nurses' station for what she hoped would be a quiet night. It never was but she still lived in hope. She was soon joined by a couple of nurses and a young doctor.

'Right,' he said, 'I'm ready to order - who wants a Chinese or pizza?'

He phoned the order through and sat down.

'This'll do me for the night.'

'Hey, you've got the only comfortable chair.'

'That's because I'm senior to you.'

'Well it's not fair.'

'You can always come and sit on my lap.'

'In your dreams.'

They laughed.

'I'll just make another check on my patients,' said Nurse Bridget. 'I'll be back by the time the pizza arrives.'

All was quiet in the ward. The only noise was coming from the giggling nurses. She picked up the pillows that

Mary Metcalfe had thrown down yet again and tried to make her comfortable. Mary wasn't having any of it and immediately threw them down again.

'Now come along Mary,' she whispered. 'I can't spend all night picking up your pillows.'

Mary grunted, but allowed herself to be propped up again.

'I'll come back later to see how you are.'

Nurse Bridget moved quietly around the ward, checking the other patients, and then returned to the nurses' station. The pizzas had arrived. The laughter and giggling continued.

The noise woke Alice Brown and, finding it difficult to go back to sleep, she got up and shuffled around the ward, finishing up at Mary Metcalfe's bed. Mary was moving about restlessly and groaning.

'Can I get you anything?'

'Get away from me, you interfering old cow. Leave me alone. I'm sick of you with your smarmy ways. You might fool them but you can't fool me. And what's more you'd better stay away from my husband if you know what's good for you.'

Suddenly she reached out, grabbed Alice's arm in a vice-like grip, dragging her closer to the bed. Alarmed, Alice fought to free herself, but Mary, fiercely strong through her anger, kept her grip. Alice called out but could not be heard above the giggling and laughter coming from the nurses' station. Mary forced Alice's face down into the pillows. Fighting to breathe, Alice flayed her arms at the air around her. Her hand came in contact with a couple of the tubes. She tugged with all her might and yanked them out of Mary's body. Mary cried out weakly, her strength quickly ebbing. She released her grip. Alice got away from her pulling the drip out as she tried to stand up. Mary fell back exhausted and breathless. Panic-stricken, Alice turned and shuffled back across the ward to the safety of her bed.

Alice was terrified. Shivering from head to foot. Her insides shook. Her teeth chattered. She managed to wrap her fleecy dressing-gown around her and lay on the bed sobbing silently. She could not believe that Mary had tried to kill her. Why would she do such a thing? What should she do? Should she call the police, doctor or nurse? Who would believe her? She was too frightened to call anyone. Too frightened to sleep. Too frightened to do anything. She lay there listening to the strange breathing noises coming from Mary until they gradually faded and eventually stopped. Exhausted, Alice fell asleep. She became aware of whispering and movement in the ward but didn't have the strength to open her eyes.

★ ★ ★

'Cup of tea, Alice? Cereal or toast?
'Tea and toast would be nice thank you.'

She sat up. Tried to avoid looking at the bed opposite but her eyes were drawn to it. Her stomach lurched and she started to shake again. The bed was empty! She didn't want to know what had happened to her, she tried to think of it as a nightmare but she heard herself asking the nurse what had happened to Mary.

'Nothing for you to worry about Alice. She has been moved to another ward. We always close this ward for the weekend. Your driver will be picking you up at 2 o'clock so you will have lunch before you go. I'll leave you a menu card. Doctor will be doing his round at 10. I'll come back to help you get into your glad rags after he has agreed that you are ready to leave us.'

A wave of relief flooded through Alice. How stupid she felt. She would have felt even more stupid if she had said anything to anyone. It had to have been a nightmare after all. She sipped her tea and ate her toast. She felt good. She felt well. She was ready to go. Then the nurse said:

'That's a nasty bruise on your arm. Who have you been fighting?' She laughed.

Alice felt faint, dizzy and sick but managed a weak laugh.

'I'm just about ready for anyone now,' she said.

★ ★ ★

Alice had been at the Cherry Trees Nursing Home for nearly two months. She still worried about that last night in the hospital but was glad that the nurse had reassured her that Mary Metcalfe was OK. She still had sleepless nights worrying that she might have murdered her but as nobody had come to arrest her she tried to dismiss the thought from her mind but couldn't. She wondered what she would do if she had. Should she confess? Should she just lie low? Meantime she had enjoyed her stay at the seaside. Everyone was good to her. Her room was lovely with a sea view. The food was great. She was feeling much stronger and able to get about but now looked forward to going home to her own little house the following week.

That afternoon Alice was disturbed and apprehensive to see Jack Metcalfe walking towards her. Oh God, what could he possibly want?

'I hope you don't mind me coming to see you here.'

'Not at all. It's a lovely surprise. Please sit down.'

'I wanted to tell you that I took your advice.'

'What advice? What advice could I have possibly given you?'

'You did. You said I should get back to doing some writing again.'

'Oh that. Oh yes so I did. So what have you been writing about?'

'Well I wrote an article and guess what! I managed to get it published in a magazine and I've brought you a copy. I hope you don't mind. I wanted to thank you in person. You helped me through the last couple of months. It's been tough since my wife died.'

'Your wife died? Oh I am sorry.'

'You didn't know?'

'No, why should I? I've been here for nearly two months.'

'It's just that she died on the day I saw you at the hospital. That is she died that same night.'

Alice stared in disbelief. All the horror of that night returned. She fought to appear outwardly calm.

'The nurse told me that she had been transferred to another ward because that ward closed for the weekend.'

'I think they say things like that to stop the other patients worrying.'

'I suppose they do.'

'It was such a shock. The doctors did all they could for her, but my silly stupid wife had only pulled out the tubes and drips. They said there was nothing much they could do except to try to make her comfortable.'

Oh my God, I really did kill her. The words rushed through her mind. She tried to concentrate. She wanted him to go away but Jack still prattled on.

'I remember you telling me that your husband died two years ago.'

'Yes, that's right.'

'How do you ever get over the loneliness? I can't get used to her not being with me.'

'You don't. You just have to get on with it and get out and about. Don't stay indoors moping. That's my advice to you.'

She wanted to have some time to sort out her thoughts and work out what she was going to do, but he carried on talking.

'May I give you my telephone number? I would love to hear from you again perhaps when you have settled back home. Maybe I could meet you for lunch or we could drive to the seaside. I know you like the coast.'

'Why not? I'd like that.'

He gave her the piece of paper with his number.

'I'd better be going now. It's been lovely to see you again. I look forward to your phone call, Alice. Bye for now.'

'Bye Jack.'

She watched him walk away along the long driveway. It seemed that with every step he took she became calmer. All the worry of the past two months lifted from her. It was, she realised, the not knowing what had happened which had caused her such distress. Now she knew. She was glad she knew. What was she going to do about it? What could she do? What was the point of doing anything? It was over.

He turned at the gate to wave goodbye. Alice waved back and thought: I wonder what he would say if I told him I'd killed his wife, and got away with it? She had to smile at that. She tore up the piece of paper with his number on it. Dropped it into the waste paper basket. Turned on the television and sat down to watch 'Midsomer Murders'.

The Best of Both Worlds
- Gloria Yeulet -

'Trevor Robinson. You are a devious and deceitful man,' said the Judge. 'I sentence you to 9 months imprisonment for perjury.'

What a thing to say about me. I can't understand it. I mean what have I done to deserve such a comment. And 9 months! I haven't committed murder. I haven't stabbed anyone or threatened anyone with menace. I haven't robbed anyone. I certainly haven't raped anyone. I haven't conned anyone out of their savings. All I did was sign my wife's name on a document, that's all. A nine month prison sentence for that.

★ ★ ★

The tide was coming in fast. So fast that Trevor was suddenly aware that the sea had surrounded the sand mound isolating him from the beach. It had deceptively crept around him, stretching, reaching out its murky brown tentacles. Drawing back, reaching out. With each movement getting closer. Stretching and reaching out to claim him as its latest victim.

★ ★ ★

Like the tide that threatened to draw me under, my life threatened to drag me down to the depths of despair.

My life had been idyllic. I had the best of both worlds one might say. Being the manager of the East Anglian region of our Estate Agency I lived at home with my wife in Essex from Friday to Monday. The rest of the week I lived with my girlfriend in a flat above one of our shops in North Norfolk. My girlfriend told me she was pregnant. Begged me to divorce my wife and marry her. She threatened to have an abortion if I didn't. How could I let her. I couldn't. So I foolishly agreed to her demand. I had no intention of leaving my wife. I had no reason. Our marriage was happy. She didn't know about my girlfriend though.

It wasn't that I had a plan or anything. It was just a stroke of luck that my wife's sister suddenly invited her to stay with her for a few weeks in her caravan on the Kent coast. It was then that the idea began to form in my mind. I could divorce my wife while she was away. She need never know. I could marry my girlfriend. Give the baby my name. Carry on living with her and my wife. In fact I could arrange for my wife and I to renew our vows in church on our wedding anniversary. Problem solved. Everyone happy. It was perfect.

I wasn't sure how to go about it so I had a word with the clerk at the courthouse. I explained that I wanted my divorce to be granted quickly as my girlfriend was pregnant and we wanted to get married before the baby was born. He was very helpful. Asked if I had been separated from my wife for more than 2 years. I admit I had to tell a little white lie. I said:

'Yes I have.'

'Then it is all straight forward. Here are the forms you need. They are a bit difficult to fill in. Would you like me to help you?'

'Yes please.'

'When the forms are processed we will send a copy to your wife for her to sign and return to the courthouse. Then I can fast forward the procedure so that you can marry your girlfriend as soon as possible. Should take about four weeks.'

'Great. Thanks for your help. I really appreciate it.'

It was that simple. I could not believe my luck.

★ ★ ★

The seawater now lapped his ankles. His feet squelched in the muddy sand. He found it difficult to keep upright. A young woman in a small rowing boat called out to him to stand by. She said she could pick him up. He waved and shouted his thanks and hoped she would hurry.

★ ★ ★

My wife returned home. She said she had a lovely time. She was thrilled when I told her I had made all the arrangements to renew our marriage vows. My girlfriend booked our wedding. Everything was wonderful until my wife's copy of the Decree Absolute was delayed because of a postal strike. It arrived while I was at work.

We could have sorted it out between ourselves. I could have explained it all to her so that she could understand why I had to do it. But oh no she had to go to the police behind my back. But that's women for you. You can't trust them and they are never satisfied. Take my girlfriend. I mean I only did it to please her. Did she appreciate it once the story appeared in the local press? She did not. Not only did she cancel the wedding she went ahead and had an abortion. I was shocked. I couldn't forgive her for doing that so I finished our relationship.

Still that was then. I've done my time. I am now free. Not only free from the prison but completely free. No ties. My wife divorced me while I was in prison. It was hard to take at the time but I've got used to it now. Unfortunately I also lost my job. That was a blow, but things are looking up. I've got several interviews lined up. One is for a job on a cruise ship. I like the sound of that.

★ ★ ★

He clambered into the small boat and saw that his rescuer was a beautiful young woman. He grinned.

'However will I be able to thank you for rescuing me?'

'I'm sure you will think of something.' She smiled at him. 'In the meantime it would help if you took the oars. It's hard work you know.'

'No use me trying to row against the tide is it? I'll just have to go with the flow.'

'Good idea. Now stop talking. Just row.'

★ ★ ★

And that's how I met Rosie. I got the job on the cruise ship as their resident dancer. My main duty is to dance with all the women who travel alone and make sure they have a wonderful holiday. I really enjoy my life aboard ship and at the end of each cruise I know that Rosie will be waiting for me. My life is once again idyllic. I have the best of both worlds one might say.